The Predators

Tombstone Jack and Thad Folger worked together at the Westfield railroads station, until Thad got fired for pilferage. Although he lost his livelihood it did not deter Folger from continuing down the road to crime with small-time thievery. He recruited the boozy Tombstone to help on a job with promises of a big take but what they find is much bigger than either could have anticipated.

When the valuable shipment destined for the army at Fort Thomas shows up missing, the army is not the only one enraged at the discovery. A gang of murderous border thugs had been hired to intercept the shipment and when they find it missing there is bloody retribution.

To find the stolen shipment two enemies, Lieutenant Calhoun and Killeen, the civilian scout must join forces when they are dispatched to track down the stolen goods and find the hideout of the notorious gang.

By the same author

The Devil's Canyon
The Drifter's Revenge
West of Tombstone
On the Wapiti Range
Rolling Thunder
The Bounty Killers
Six Days to Sundown
Saddle Tramps
The Shadow Riders
The Outpost
Quinn's Last Run
Ransom
Long Blows the North Wind
The Highwaymen

The Predators

Owen G. Irons

ROBERT HALE · LONDON

First published in Great Britain 2011

ISBN 978-0-7090-9124-0

Robert Hale Limited
Clerkenwell House
Clerkenwell Green
London EC1R 0HT

www.halebooks.com

Typeset by
Derek Doyle & Associates, Shaw Heath
Printed and bound in Great Britain by
CPI Antony Rowe, Chippenham and Eastbourne

ONE

'Predatory,' Tombstone Jack said removing his hat to scratch at his thinly-thatched head. 'I recognize the word, but I can't seem to find a home for it.'

Thaddeus Folger crouched down beside Jack in the ribbon of shade cast by the railroad depot's awning. Glancing up the long silver rails of track stretching to the prairie horizon, he explained, 'It's a matter of the railroad company paying us for what they've taken from us.'

'They never took nothin' from me,' Jack replied, 'Except once when the vice-president of the line was due to come through on an inspection, Garrett took my whiskey flask away.'

'That's what I mean!' Thad Folger said loudly. He took Tombstone Jack by the lapels of his shabby tweed coat and drew him nearer. 'They are downright predatory. They took what was yours, deprived you of your small comfort. They had no right to do that – anymore than they've had the right to take away your pride, to rob you of your proper position in life, to deny you your just desserts.'

'You're talking about them firing you, aren't you?' Jack said, removing Thad's clutching fingers from his lapels.

'Well . . . yes, that is one more example of their brazen disregard for their employees' God-given rights.'

'You were skunking away a crate of goods about every night that you were standing watch,' Jack reminded Thad Folger. 'Hardware, tinned food, dress fabric. . . .'

'Only because they refused to pay me a living wage!' Folger replied indignantly. 'I was balancing the scales of injustice. A man has the right to lead a life of reasonable comfort.'

'What you are really getting to – the long way around – is that you want me to help you rob the railroad,' Jack said, cutting to the heart of the matter.

'What I am saying,' Thad Folger answered without abandoning his virtuous stance, 'is that the railroad has put me in a position where I have no other choice but to seek redress. I was meanly treated. You, Jack, what have you left for your old age? I'll tell you: nothing. Not even the memory of a well-spent and comfortably-rewarded life.'

'That's enough of this talk,' Jack said, holding up a gnarled hand to fend off Folger's cascade of words. 'If you want me to help you hijack freight off the six-o'clock train, just say so!'

'You have the right. . . !'

'Maybe, maybe not. Anyway, I could use the money,' Jack replied, rubbing his bristly chin.

'That's it,' Colin Babbit said. 'They're coming in on the six o'clock train for a certainty.' Henry Crimson, still looking doubtful, took the yellow Western Union telegram Babbit had placed on the banker's desk and studied it.

'Are you sure you can trust this Pierce Avery?'

'Absolutely. We rode a lot of trails together before he got himself thrown off his horse and broke his leg. I told you, he's the yard boss at the freight office in Tamarind Springs. He knows everything that is loaded on the trains down to the last nail.'

Henry Crimson leaned back in his green leather office chair and scratched at the back of his head, barely disturbing his pomaded hair which was parted in the middle. The banker smiled – or

Babbit thought it was an attempt at a smile and his small blue eyes brightened behind the rimless bifocals he wore.

'There's a lot of money to be made in rifles,' the banker said thoughtfully, now studying the narrow face of his potential partner. Babbit wore a full reddish mustache and it twitched now as he agreed with the banker.

'You bet there is.'

The guns in question were the brand new Winchester '73s being freighted to nearby Fort Thomas to replace the outdated .45-70 Springfields the army had been using for years. The breech-loaders were slow to load and had long been obsolete. The War Department, it seemed, had belatedly come to recognize that, and was now prepared to arm their cavalry soldiers in the Western lands with modern weapons. This was the first shipment of the new rifles.

'Will you need help?' Henry Crimson asked.

'Of course I will. Those rifle crates will be heavy. I'll need a few strong men, a wagon to haul them away. Maybe a place to stash them until the heat is off.' Colin Babbit was leaning on the banker's desk now, his face intent. He desperately needed money. He was not much younger than Pierce Avery had been when he had shattered his leg in three places and found he would no longer be able to hit the trail. That he had found a job working for the railroad had been a boon for Pierce, but it didn't pay much, and certainly the sedentary life of an office worker did not appeal to Colin Babbit. He needed to make his score, and now.

He had suggested the idea to Crimson one night in the Starshine Saloon. Both men were heavy drinkers, and Babbit had merely been looking for sympathy, maybe a suggestion. He had not known that Henry Crimson had been chipping away at the bank's money for years and lived in constant fear of the territorial bank examiner finding out about it. It meant prison for sure unless he could find a way to replace the stolen funds.

Crimson had built a fine frame house for his chubby bride and indulged her beyond his salary. It wasn't so much his own humiliation that would trouble him if he were arrested for embezzlement, but what Lena would have to endure, since the town's ladies would surely ostracize her if Crimson were ever found out, and Lena took great pride in her position as one of the town's leading matrons. One reason she had married the banker in the first place.

'You know reliable men you can hire for the job?' Henry Crimson asked.

'I think so. Of course we'll have to give them something in advance.'

'Give me a price, Babbit. I'll take care of that end of things.' After all, what did a few dollars more matter now? He had already dug himself a hole too deep to crawl out of, and this promised to be a redemption – if Colin Babbit could pull it off.

'I was thinking that we should hit the train when it stopped at Comanche Wells for water. We sure can't rob the train right here in Westfield, not with the whole town looking. We'd be sure to be seen and there would likely be a gunfight.'

'No, that's no good,' the banker agreed hastily. 'Not in town, of course not. If you think Comanche Wells is the place. . . .'

'It is. There's flat land for miles around. The only people living there are the station master and a few jackrabbits,' Colin said, trying for some humor to ease the tension which had been growing in the room. Now that the plan had been agreed to and established, both men knew that they were in too deep to pull out. If they failed they would have the law and the US Army as pursuers. It was a desperate plan, but Babbit could find no flaw in it. Out on the open plains, the train stopped for water for its boiler, would be an easy target. Babbit had already checked with Pierce Avery – there would be no passenger cars attached, so they didn't have to concern themselves with some unexpectedly bold traveler taking a hand.

'Find some men,' Henry Crimson said, rising. The banker was taller than he seemed seated behind his desk. Arrow-thin, he and his somewhat pudgy wife were quite a sight when they went out walking and more than a few jokes had been made behind their backs. 'And,' Crimson added, readjusting his spectacles, 'make sure they're tough enough for the job. When you've done that and located a wagon, come back here and tell me how much money you'll need to carry matters through.'

Babbit left without having shaken hands, and from his office window, Crimson could see the old trailsman striding down the main street toward the nearest saloon. He wished that things had not come this far, to the point where he was actually soliciting a criminal enterprise, but then again he had done it to himself. Not out of greed, he told himself, but out of love. His explanation did not stand up to self-examination in the brilliant light the desert sun beamed through his window. Sighing heavily he seated himself again. A few local ranchers had applied for loans lately, and he was going to have to turn them down. Not because he didn't trust them, but only because he had frittered away a good portion of the bank's money.

Babbit's scheme had to work.

'What do you figure,' Tombstone Jack was asking Thad Folger.

'It's nearly dusk at six o'clock, this time of the year. The train will be stopping for about an hour to let the crew step down and grab some supper. There shouldn't be anyone around – a few idlers and kids who like to watch the trains come and go, but outside of that, no one.

'We pull a railroad freight truck up on the opposite side of the train and take what we can find and move quickly. Last week I got a shipment of ready-made town suits,' Folger said, his voice lowering to a cunning whisper. 'Sold them to the dry goods store on the cheap. They got a bargain; I got some good money out of it.'

'We should be so lucky this time,' Tombstone Jack said a little worriedly.

'It'll work fine,' Folger said, slapping Jack on the shoulder. 'If anyone sees you, they all know you work here. Who would question you? Is Garrett around that late?' he inquired. The station master was a concern.

'No, he knocks off at five and goes home to dinner unless there's something important going on,' Jack answered.

'Outside of the marshal, there's no one to worry about. Does Slattery ever come down here?'

'To watch the trains?' Jack asked. 'Why? It's the railroad's business, not his.' Besides, he thought, the fat town marshal hated even to lift himself out of his office chair for any reason. 'No, he won't be around.'

'And Jack, the railroad won't even know that anything is missing until it reaches the end of the line. That's how I've gotten away with it this long.'

'I still don't like this much,' Tombstone Jack said.

'But you're going through with it?' Thad Folger asked a little anxiously.

'Yes, I guess I am,' Jack drawled.

'We'll need at least six men,' Colin Babbit was saying in a near whisper as he sat in the Starshine Saloon across the table from Trevor Steele. 'And a wagon.'

Trevor Steele had listened to Babbit's plan with doubt and then with unexpressed eagerness. *Rifles*! He could use them for sure.

'How can you be sure that the rifles are really on board?' Steele asked and Babbit once more told the story of Pierce Avery, the man at the Tamarind Springs freight office.

'And you trust him?' Steele asked, biting at his lower lip.

'Yes. He's my friend, an old trail partner.' Babbit smiled thinly, 'And I promised him a cut of the profit.'

That was the same reason he was counting on Steele. The man had been known to do most anything for money. And Trevor Steele had a dozen tough men at his beck and call, waiting just for moments like this.

'Comanche Wells, you figure?' Steele asked thoughtfully. 'Yes, I guess that is the place to hit the train. No citizens, no law around for miles.'

'I'm going to start that way with a wagon as soon as I can rent one,' Babbit said.

'Hold on,' Steele said as Babbit started to rise. 'You haven't told me who was going to pay my men?'

'You don't need to know. Just tell me how much you want and I'll see that you have it within the hour.'

'All right,' Steele said unhappily. He liked to know the people he was working with. For one thing, that sort of information might come in handy later. He quoted what seemed an exorbitant price for his services and scribbled the number down on a scrap of paper in case Babbit's memory faltered.

Babbit stared at the pencil. Steele wrote the numbers as if using a carving knife. 'No less, you understand?' he asked with a veiled threat.

'I'll get it,' Colin Babbit said uneasily, folding the paper and placing it in his shirt pocket. He hoped that Henry Crimson didn't balk when he saw the figure. But Babbit had the idea that Crimson wasn't using his own money for the operation anyway. Stepping outside into the harsh daylight, Babbit glanced at his steel pocket watch. There should be time to beat the train to Comanche Wells if he kept moving.

Fifteen minutes later Babbit was at the Trail's End Stable, bargaining with the owner. Crimson had handed over the money without a comment, but his face, set into an unhappy scowl, revealed a sort of desperation. When Babbit had tracked down Trevor Steele standing at the bar of the Starshine talking to a pair of rough-looking bearded men – part of the crew he was assembling? – he motioned with his head and Steele followed him outside to accept the packet of currency, flipping through it casually before tucking it away in the pocket of his gray, tailored coat.

'The train should reach Comanche Wells a little after seven. It'll be coming on to full dark by then. If you cut through the rocky pass along the Pine

Bluff you can be there well ahead of it, soon enough to choose your positions, take care of the station master and the train crew.'

'I know what I'm doing,' Trevor Steele said. 'Just make sure you're there with that wagon.'

'Mr Steele,' Colin Babbit asked with some concern, 'are you sure you can gather six men in time?'

Steele laughed. 'I can get men to work for me at the drop of a hat,' he boasted.

Babbit hoped he was right, because there wasn't any time to waste.

Now as he dickered with Wally Shoup, the owner of the Trail's End, over a wagon which Shoup could not know that Babbit would have rented at any price, Colin Babbit for the first time began to feel nervous. The planning had been by far the easy part. The execution of the plan would take luck and nerve. Babbit had had a pretty rough life, but he was no natural criminal.

'This is the last usable wagon I have around,' Shoup was saying. A thin, red-headed man he had a cheek full of tobacco as always. He spat. 'Not an hour ago Tombstone Jack came by and. . . .'

'I'll take it,' Colin Babbit said more loudly than he intended. He had no wish to hear the details of Shoup's business day.

After selecting two sturdy-appearing bay horses to pull the wagon, they went into Shoup's closet-sized office and Babbit paid the rental fee. Babbit's hands trembled anxiously as he counted out the money, but Shoup apparently did not notice. His eyes were only on the currency being dealt out on his desk.

Shoup helped Babbit harness and hitch the horses to the wagon and then sauntered back into the shadowed stable while Babbit started on his way beneath the high, white sun toward Comanche Wells.

'Did you get the wagon?' Thad Folger asked Tombstone Jack.

'Sure did. It's on the side of the depot, next to the railroad trucks,' Jack said. 'No one will think anything about it, figuring it's someone come to pick up their freight.'

'And so it is,' Thad Folger replied with a sly smile.

Tombstone Jack was looking a little unsettled. He fidgeted, glanced at his watch – five o'clock – and fidgeted some more. 'This is going to work, isn't it, Thad?'

'It will. It has to.'

Otherwise they would find themselves sharing time in the territorial prison. Thad couldn't really see how things could go wrong. Marshal Slattery wouldn't be around. He had never come down to the depot before. There would be no passengers and no railroad guards simply because there was no place for them to ride, and it was only freight, anyway. Gold shipments had extra protection, but this was not gold, only shipments of odds and ends to settlers on the far plains. Thad had managed to make a small if steady profit off such goods before he was fired from the railroad, and he had made a few contacts. Merchants who were not particular about where their stores came from.

'Good thing you work here,' Folger commented to Tombstone Jack. 'Otherwise we couldn't get away with it.'

'Well, I might not be working here anymore after today, right?'

'They'll never know where they lost the freight,' Folger said. 'Could be at any one of half a dozen stops along the line. You're safe.'

'What do we take?' Tombstone Jack asked.

'Whatever's closest to the door and easy to unload. We don't want to be around the train any longer than necessary. Put a smile on your face, Tombstone! When I was working here, I pulled this off three times a week or more.'

'Until they caught you.'

'They never caught me!' Folger answered with

resentment. 'They only *suspected* me. That's what I was talking about, you see? How can they fire a man from his job only on suspicion? That's what should be a crime.

'And if I am a criminal – well they made me one. When I lost my job, I had no other way to go.'

Tombstone Jack had heard this same complaint, or variations of it a dozen times. It always amazed him that Thad Folger was able to dredge up real indignation when he told it. Jack settled on to the bench in front of the depot, legs stretched out, watching for the six o'clock train.

TWO

The station master, Quentin Garrett, locked his office door at precisely five o'clock and started home. His wife had a standing order that Garrett adhere to his schedule. She would have one of her tasteless suppers, always served with over-boiled potatoes, waiting for him when he reached home and then he would spend an enjoyable evening watching her knit. The truth was Garrett was happiest when he was at the station. There things were always in motion and he was in charge. However, the six o'clock was not a passenger train, but only a freight and it was not even unloading anything at this stop and he could be of no possible use.

The railroad crew would step down, stretch and take their meal over at the Bluebird Café. Tombstone Jack would chase off any kid who wanted to climb aboard the locomotive – he was good for that much at least. He spotted the idler sitting on the bench at the side of the depot as he passed. For this Jack was paid? Truthfully, Garrett knew, there was little for Jack to be doing either except keeping an eye on things. At least Garrett didn't spot that thief Thad Folger lurking around; apparently he had taken Garrett's warning to stay well clear of the tracks to heart. Quentin Garrett plodded home, realizing that there was only so much a man could do to keep his world organized. Fate always took a hand.

The freight train pulled in with a clank and a shriek of brakes, a ringing of its bell and a puff of expelled steam at five minutes to six. Tombstone Jack rose to his feet with the anxiety of anticipation, walking the length of the platform and back several times. Then he seated himself again to wait.

After a few more minutes Thad Folger slipped out of the forming shadows striding toward Jack.

'Get up! I saw Gallett headed home earlier. Is the train crew gone?'

'Five minutes ago, walking toward the Bluebird.'

'Anyone else around?'

'The usual bunch of kids. I'll shoo them off and we can get started.'

'Leave that. It doesn't matter. We'll be on the far side of the train, besides the kids don't know what our business here is. I doubt many people even know that I've been fired. It'll just seem that we're doing our job.'

'If you say so,' Tombstone said doubtfully. 'Let's get it done quick, though.'

'I've already brought the truck around from the barn. Let's get it across the tracks.'

The high-wheeled, stake-bed wagon was painted green with yellow wheels. Designed only for transferring luggage and freight from one end of the platform to the other, it didn't take much to tow it; however on the opposite side of the tracks the ground sloped away and it would take the two of them to manage it.

The light in the sky was dimming. There was a vaguely purple band along the western horizon. The train had three freight cars attached and Tombstone Jack asked, 'Which one do you want to open.'

Straining to keep the baggage cart from slipping away down the slope, Thad Folger panted an answer, 'It doesn't matter. The nearest one, I suppose.'

The truck had no brake – one wasn't normally needed, and so they chocked the wheels with a few rocks, enough to keep it stationary on the slight incline. Looking around with some trepidation, Tombstone Jack climbed on to the heavy cart, looking up and down the tracks. He clipped the wire seal from the freight car with a tool he carried for that purpose and opened the heavy door of the freight car. It slid along its tracks with a squeal and a groan which seemed unnaturally loud to Tombstone. He looked up and down the tracks again before slipping inside. Standing there he looked around. There were barrels, presumably of nails, many unlabeled crates.

'What do we take?' he asked Thad in an overly loud hiss.

'Whatever's nearest. We've got to keep this short.'

The crates nearest Tombstone had stencils reading 'Ironware'. He eyed these dubiously, but Thad, standing behind him on the bed of the wagon said:

'That's fine. Slide those over here.'

'Ironware?'

'That could be anything. Maybe stove parts, kettles, frying pans. There's always a market for those. A lot of settlers dumped that stuff on the way west to lighten their wagons when they hit a long grade. They're at a premium out here. Shove them over.'

There were three of them, and Tombstone, energized by unease, slid them to Thad Folger in rapid order. As Thad dragged the crates backward by their rope handles, Tombstone Jack lowered the other ends on to the wagon bed.

'Come on,' Folger said, 'keep moving. Those railroaders are fast eaters.'

In quick succession then they took a crate labeled 'cotton bolts' which pleased Thad. 'The ladies always want new cloth.' Two anonymous-looking smaller boxes which might have contained anything, and later proved to be clocks, and five carefully packed glass panes followed. Thad decided that was enough. He was even more nervous than Tombstone although he had been in the business longer.

'Let's get going, Jack. We've gotten a few hundred dollars out of this night's work.'

'All right. Is our wagon hitched?' he asked as he slipped out of the car and slid the complaining door of the freight car shut again, re-wrapping the wire so that a casual eye could not tell that it had been tampered with.

'It's standing at the side of the freight house. Let's keep moving.'

Pushing, pulling and heaving, they managed to get the truck up the slope and across the tracks to the platform just as the returning railroad men came into sight.

'Let's get this out of here!' Folger said, his nerves obviously giving way. They made it around the corner of the depot just as the fireman, brakeman and engineer reached the locomotive and mounted the iron steps.

'That was pretty close,' Tombstone Jack said.

'As close as I want to get. We knew we didn't have much time, but that's not a bad haul for half an hour's work,' Thad said, nodding at the high hand truck they had paused to rest against. After a few minutes of deep breathing, they heard the locomotive's boiler building up steam and Thad said, 'Come on, we're not through yet.'

The bed of the freight truck did not match up well with that of the rented wagon. It stood about eighteen inches higher. The crates slid off with unnerving thuds in the silence of the evening, but the loading did not take long. Tombstone threw a tarp over the stolen goods as Thad wheeled the railroad truck to its usual position beside the depot.

Returning, he stepped up into the wagon box, taking the reins from Jack.

'We don't have to go far,' Thad told Tombstone Jack. 'I rented that disused barn at the edge of town from Paulsen. He was happy to get something for the place. I've been sleeping there too,' Thad Folger said with an edge of bitterness creeping into his voice.

It was the first indication Tombstone Jack had had that perhaps Folger wasn't doing as well at this racket as he had pretended. He only nodded a response, wondering all the while if he had been stupid risking his steady if low-paying job to become an outlaw who might be worse paid. *Just this one time,* Jack told himself as they headed toward the barn through an oak grove, following a little-used trail north of town.

The barn was of weathered gray wood and seemed to tilt a little. There were boards nailed across the hayloft window in an 'X' and as he found out when they stepped down, a new hasp lock on the double doors in front.

'My warehouse!' Thad Folger said expansively as they stepped inside the crumbling barn and Thad lit a lantern which had been hanging on a nail near the door. Tombstone didn't know if Thad had been hoping to impress him or was trying to bolster his own sense of worth. There was little to be seen – a few wooden crates which had been breached, three or four readymade suits hanging on a makeshift rack, a few ladies' hats on a shelf, a box of chipped dishes, a stack of blankets. Tombstone only nodded.

'Not bad.'

'Oh, there's not much left here, and I'll tell you why, Jack – I've got merchants just begging for everything I bring in. I move my goods out almost as quick as I can bring them in.'

'That's something,' Jack said. He had noticed the old army cot in the corner. Apparently that was where Thad was sleeping these days. It made Tombstone Jack appreciate his little bed over at the boarding house.

'Now,' Thad Folger said, rubbing his hands together eagerly. 'Let's see what we've brought in tonight.'

They backed the wagon into the musty interior of the old barn and began unloading. The bolts of material and the glass panes were on top along with the smaller boxes. These they opened to discover brass-bound wall clocks.

'That fabric can be sold tomorrow, I promise you,' Thad said, although Jack wondered exactly how much it was worth. 'The glass will go – glass is always at a premium. Dowd at the hardware store will leap at the chance to buy it.'

Yes, maybe, Jack reflected. Glass was certainly hard to come by, but there were only five panes in various sizes, obviously intended for a specific purpose farther along the line. It was all saleable merchandise, but hardly the bonanza Thad had been promising.

'OK – let's get that ironware down and see what we've got,' Folger said.

What they had was trouble.

No sooner had they muscled the first of the three crates down than Thad went at it with his crowbar. Popping the lid he blinked, stood up and stepped back, his eyes wide. Inside the crate, packed in heavy yellow waxed paper and cosmoline were a dozen factory-new Winchester '73s.

The other two crates were unloaded and lowered to the ground quickly, their lids pried open. They were all the same. Three dozen rifles, obviously a delivery meant for the army.

'Holy smoke!' Thad Folger said. 'Do you know what we've got here? A small fortune!'

To Tombstone Jack they still looked like trouble.

By the time the locomotive had built up a head of steam and was drawing out of the Westfield station, Trevor Steele was already on the trail, well ahead of it, heading for the Pine Bluff cut-off. It was a much shorter route to Comanche Wells, but very steep for a train even if the railroad had wanted to waste the months of effort to blast the rock and try building a trestle over the river.

With Steele were five hand-picked men, riding silently through the twilight. They would reach the Comanche Wells station in plenty of time to take care of the station master and anyone else who might be around, find their positions and await the train carrying the new army rifles. It didn't seem like that much of a haul to his hired men, but Steele knew places where he could easily get upwards of $500 for each of the new weapons. Of course, eventually they would become commonplace and their price would drop like a stone, but that was in the future, and for the time being the Winchester '73s could be no more valuable that if they were made of gold.

Your adversary, if he was carrying a .45-70, fired one round before reloading. Even if he was carrying one of those older Spencer .56 repeaters which first saw use in the Civil War, he had only five shots. There were still a few of the obsolete 1865 models floating around, mostly carried by men who had used them during the war, but that .56 caliber ammunition was getting scarce. With a Winchester, depending on the configuration, you had up to fifteen shots and rechambering a fresh cartridge took only a flick of the lever, and they took the .44-40 cartridge, which was plentiful no matter where you were riding, it being the same caliber Colt revolvers were chambered for.

Yes, in certain quarters with which Steele was well familiar, they were worth that much money. Trevor Steele also meant to keep one for his own use.

Colin Babbit's contact in Tamarind hadn't been certain of the number of individual weapons the train was actually carrying. After all the man could hardly pry open a crate to examine them, but he had told Babbit that there were three crates. Steele guessed that depending on how they were packed that was somewhere between thirty and fifty Winchesters. He did the math as his horse jolted on, beginning the ascent of the Pine Bluff trail.

It would be enough to make it well worth his while.

Colin Babbit had driven his rented wagon away from the Trail's End Stable at about five o'clock. He already felt guilty. Passing Quentin Garrett and Marshal Slattery who were standing on the board-walk, exchanging pleasantries, it seemed to Babbit that both men turned suspicious eyes his way.

Imagination, of course. A man had the right to rent a wagon in Westfield, didn't he! Well, not if his intent was to transport a load of stolen army rifles. Was it his conscience that was bothering him? No, it was strictly fear of being caught, and these were not the same thing.

Colin Babbit tugged the brim of his hat lower and set out to chase the setting sun toward Comanche Wells.

Trevor Steele halted his men for a few minutes as they achieved the flats of Pine Bluff. There was still plenty of time and he wanted the horses rested when they reached Comanche Wells. He expected no trouble, but had not survived all those years as a border bandit without anticipating the possibility of trouble. Those had not been pleasant years, constantly getting shot at, enduring the long trail with the cut-throats he was forced to associate with. Gradually, Steele had climbed to the top of the pyramid partly because of his organizing, partly through the use of his own learned brutality. For five years he had led the border raiders.

One day his age seemed suddenly to catch up with him, and he found that he had lost his darker ambitions. Before he could be displaced forcefully, Steele had decided to retire, handing over leadership of the gang to Alberto Mingo. Steele had moved to Westfield, visited a barber and a tailor and settled into a new life – still without a bullet hole in his body.

Only a few men in Westfield knew of his past.

Marshal Slattery was not one of them. The fat marshal seemed unaware of anything that went on outside of his office, and that suited Steele well as he settled into the life of a gambler, only occasionally returning to his outlaw ways. Lately, he had been having a run of bad luck at the faro table, and this opportunity had come along at the right time.

Steele reflected that it did not even cost him a thing to try. Some unknown backer had paid the men he now rode with. The rest was pure profit, as he had no intention of splitting the final take with his riders. They had been paid; they had agreed to the terms.

Nor did he have any intention of splitting the profit with his backer – Steele who had feelers out everywhere, was certain he knew who the money man was, and that person could not and would not complain if he didn't get his share. Mingo would take the rifles off his hands and be glad to get them no matter the price, and Steele already had an exorbitant figure in mind. Mingo, he knew, had been doing quite well lately; supplying his men with new Winchesters would be to his advantage.

Any way Steele looked at it, it was pure profit with little risk.

'Let's ride, men!' he shouted, stepping into leather himself. It was still a long ride to Comanche

Wells, and a few minutes earlier he had heard the distant whistle of the freight train as it drew out of the station at Westfield.

The men Trevor Steele had gathered for this raid were all well-known to him – with one exception. Two of them were former border raiders themselves. A couple were army deserters. The one man he did not know was a clean-shaven pockmarked man named Ben Curry. Curry had the hungry aspect of a slinking coyote. Steele wouldn't have chosen the man himself, but Bill Vaughn, a man he knew from his past, vouched for him, and Steele had felt that he needed one more rider. Steele didn't like the looks Curry shot his way, but it didn't matter much. Curry had been hired on for one day's work. Steele didn't take the time to speculate on where the man had come from or what his ambitions were. He was simply another tool as all the riders in his border army had been. Steele was not a man to form close attachments.

He had liked Alberto Mingo, but that perhaps was because the raider had always been respectful, always did his work without complaint, rather than out of any personal feelings he held. Besides, it would be risky indeed for anyone – Steele included – ever to cross Alberto Mingo. Their business association was now over. Mingo had gotten what he wanted, Steele what he wished.

Now what Steele wanted was to sell Mingo the new rifles for a tidy profit. He saw no problem there. Mingo had the money, and he always wanted more firepower. Well, he was about to get it. Comanche Wells, what there was of it, appeared on the broad plains ahead.

THREE

Colin Babbit was walking the team of horses drawing the rented wagon. He saw no need to hurry, even though he could hear the near whistle of the approaching locomotive. He would be there in plenty of time; what he wanted to avoid was any possible gunfire if someone decided to try to stand up before Trevor Steele. That seemed unlikely. So far as Babbit knew there was only the station master, an older, partially crippled man and his assistant who worked the water tower, a young, half-bright kid. Nor could Babbit see the railroad crew opening up with their guns – probably none of them even carried a weapon.

The station was small, square and dilapidated although it could have been built no more than five years earlier when the Arizona & Eastern had first developed this spur, primarily to serve Fort Thomas. The harsh conditions out here could age structures prematurely – women and men as well, Babbit reflected.

As he guided the team pulling his wagon forward, he thought he had a glimpse of a body of men – shadows against the plains – approaching the station from the east. It could be, had to be, Trevor Steele and his men. Far away he again heard the hooting of a train whistle, presumably sounded to let the station master at the water stop know it was arriving, although Babbit saw no one moving in front of the station nor around the water tower. Perhaps they knew how much time they had to prepare things.

Babbit's stomach had begun to clench, his mouth to develop a sour taste, suddenly he had no liking for this. He was among dangerous men. If he could, he thought he would have changed his mind and simply driven away. But it was too late in the game. He had already taken money from Henry Crimson. And he now had Trevor Steele as a partner in the enterprise. Neither would accept failure. No, he was in too deep now. He had to follow the plan to the bitter end.

Ross McCoy emerged from the tiny railroad depot

and peered Indian-style to the south, shading his eyes with his hand. Although dusk was settling rapidly, there was still a flare of yellow light beaming through a notch in the western mountains. He glanced at his watch. Right on time.

'Charles!' he shouted back at the building. 'It's time!'

McCoy limped along the narrow platform of the building and waited for Charles who would have to lower the spout and fill the locomotive's boiler with water. That job took some effort and McCoy was no longer young or spry. Charles was like a little monkey, eager to please, clever at his single job. It was about all the poor boy was clever at, but both of them were lucky to have each other at this point in their lives. Neither could have functioned long without the other's help.

Now, as the brilliant sunlight through the notch faded to darkness and the sky purpled, McCoy could see the train approaching, its bulk massive, its drive wheels churning powerfully. McCoy loved the trains. The swiftness, the metallic energy. They were a wonder. The diamond stack of the locomotive blew white smoke now as it rushed across the plains toward Comanche Wells. His job was to nourish the engine, to provide it with water as it dashed on across the long grass plains toward distant destinations. McCoy felt proud and protective. The railroad was his way of life. He was a midwife to the birth of a new West.

Just for a moment he thought he saw movement off to the east. A few men on horseback approaching the station. They could be anyone. When the train was towing passenger cars sometimes the surrounding ranchers would bring someone – wife, daughter, son – over to Comanche Wells to board the train for some distant place. But this was a freight train only, McCoy knew.

As Charles brushed past him, heading eagerly toward the water tank, McCoy's seamed face formed itself into a frown. When he made out two more riders approaching the station through the darkness he retreated toward the open door of the station and retrieved his shotgun leaning against the wall there.

In the early days he had kept it always handy. You never knew when a band of Indians might take a notion to have a look at what the train was carrying. Sometimes they rode away with trophies; sometimes finding nothing of use, they left unwanted goods strewn across the plains. After the second time the Indians had come, McCoy had started carrying the shotgun every time a train arrived.

Lately he had given up the habit, but now as he

saw six men riding steadily toward the station, he decided that bringing out the twelve-gauge might only be due caution.

McCoy returned to the platform. Now he could see, to the south, a man driving a wagon toward Comanche Wells. And the wagon was empty – he could see that much, and his suspicions deepened. The train was approaching at a crawl now, drive wheels back-turning, the brakes screeching as the engineer began to position the locomotive beneath the spout of the water tank.

McCoy limped toward the locomotive. Looking up into the cab he saw that it was Frank Ames driving. McCoy stepped up on to the lowest step of the locomotive and said to Ames.

'Be wary, Frank. Something may be up.'

Ames nodded. He had seen much in his ten years on the line and he knew that McCoy was not given to hysterics. He frowned and nodded, opening the iron box in the locomotive cab where three holstered Colt .44 pistols were kept. Two of these he handed to his fireman and brakeman; the other he belted on as they watched young Charlie pull the guide wire and lower the spout of the fill pipe to the boiler reservoir.

'What's up?' Joe Cox the fireman asked, buckling on his own pistol.

'I don't know,' Ames replied. 'Something has McCoy spooked.'

That was good enough for Cox who opened the loading gate on his Colt and checked his cartridges. There was nothing, no one to be seen moving in the near-darkness although Cox could swear that he heard horses shuffling their feet somewhere beyond the station.

Ames, who was also listening intently, thought he heard the sound of an approaching wagon's ungreased axles complaining. Not Indians, then, he thought. They had had little trouble with them since Fort Thomas had been built. No, this was something else.

Trevor Steele had expected no trouble at Comanche Wells, and he confidently led his men forward now as the train sat still, straddling its tracks: a gigantic beast catching its breath. They rounded the corner of the depot in a line, and a voice rang out.

'Hold it there, gents!'

What the hell! Steele reached for his sidearm as did Bill Vaughan beside him. Before either man had cleared leather, a shotgun blast, ferociously loud in the night, sounded and Bill was blown from his saddle. Steele jerked his horse's head away as the second load in the shotgun was fired. Angry now, Steele shouted out, 'Shoot anything that moves, boys!'

McCoy feared for a few moments that he had acted precipitously, but that thought was quickly banished as half a dozen weapons opened up from out of the darkness. Bullets rang off the side of the depot, whined off the steelworks of the locomotive. It was like being in a war zone. Running as rapidly as his damaged leg would allow back toward the station to gather more shotgun shells, McCoy felt hot lead riddle his body and he fell face first to the planks of the depot platform. Charles watched uncomprehendingly from his position at the base of the wooden water tower. He rushed to aid McCoy – his only friend – and was cut down by a dozen bullets.

In the cab of the locomotive, Ames ducked down behind the steel skirt surrounding it as lead bullets splatted against the steel or sang off in ricochets. The brakeman, Walter Cannon, stood up and tried to exchange fire with the raiders and was immediately cut down to lay bleeding against the iron floor of the cab.

'We can't win!' Joe Cox, the fireman screamed at Ames.

He was right, of course. Frank Ames's job was to

drive the train, to protect it as well as possible, but they were being swarmed by hostile gunfire and the railroad could not reasonably expect them to do more. He gave it up.

'We've had enough!' he shouted at the darkness, and he and Joe Cox flung their handguns out of the cab.

The gunfire abated, stopped. Finally a deep voice called out. 'Step down, boys. We've nothing against you.'

A little sheepishly Ames and Cox stepped down from the cab, hands hoisted high, their holsters empty. There were four men waiting to surround them when they reached the ground. One – their leader – demanded:

'Where are those army rifles?'

'Last car,' Ames said without hesitation. Let them have the rifles, anything they wanted. He just wanted to get rolling again and live to see his wife and daughters. They heard Steele giving orders.

'The man says the last car! Break it open, boys. Where's that wagon? We may be out on the plains, but someone might have heard us. Let's keep moving!'

From the corner of his eye as his men popped the wire seal on the freight car door, Steele saw the wagon driven by Colin Babbit pulling up. Right on time. This was going to work out perfectly. A man called Waco yelled out to Steele in frustration from the freight car.

'They're not in here, Steele!'

Steele winced. He did not like his name being called out in the hearing of the train men. He challenged the coverall-clad Frank Ames. 'The man says the rifles aren't in the last car.'

Ames, cowed, but angry, snapped, 'Well, I don't know where the hell they are. It's not my job to keep track of the freight.'

'All right,' Steele said placatingly. The engineer was not lying; why would he? Steele shouted out: 'Pop them all open. We know those rifles are on board somewhere!'

Or did they? He glared at Colin Babbit who had stepped down from his wagon's bench seat to stretch. They were working under an assumption presented by Babbit. Without speaking aloud, Steele made his thoughts known. *They had better be on this train.*

What a misfortune it would be to be sent to prison for a train robbery without even having profited from it. Lately, the laws against train robbery had been strengthened, the penalties stiffened. It was twenty-five years at the least if convicted, and these train men had seen Steele's face and even heard his name shouted out. That was all right – Trevor Steele had lived on the run before, and he had his hideouts in Mexico. So long as it was not all for nothing!

Still holding his gun leveled on the engineer and his companion, Steele glanced along the length of the train to see his men were crawling into all three freight cars, searching for the Winchester repeaters.

His *three* men, Steele reflected. Bill Vaughan and one of the army deserters, Peach, had both been killed in the initial assault. He was left with only Waco, Tom Bull and Curry. If you didn't count Colin Babbit, which Steele didn't. If his information had been wrong, Babbit might not matter to anyone anymore before this evening was done.

'There's nothing!' Waco called from the second car in line. The robbers had begun throwing unwanted goods out on the ground in a manner which made the Indians look respectful.

'Where are they?' Steele demanded coldly, placing the muzzle of his Colt revolver directly under the engineer's nose and nudging it a little.

Frank Ames answered in a strangled snarl. 'I've told you all I know. My job's to drive the train, not to load the freight.'

Steele, recognizing the truth in what the engineer said, lowered his pistol. It appeared now that they had been given the wrong information. Judging by the amount of freight strewn alongside the train track, the freight cars had been nearly emptied. He wheeled angrily on the nearby Colin Babbit, but was interrupted by Waco who was approaching. Waco was wafer-thin, blond, as sincere as a border outlaw can be.

'Boss,' he announced, 'I thought I should speak up. The third car, the one where the weapons were supposed to be – I'm pretty sure someone had jimmied it open before we got to work on it. I mean, the other two cars we had to clip the wire seal, but the last car only had a twist in the wire to secure it.'

'Someone else has been in it?' Steele asked.

'Looked that way to me. I thought I'd better say something.'

Steele turned again to Babbit, his wrath somewhat cooled. 'What do you know about this?' Trevor Steele demanded.

Colin Babbit found his knees wobbling as he faced Steele's anger. *Never again*, he swore in silence. Never again would he become involved in anything like this. Casting about mentally for a way to deflect Steele's fury, he came upon a memory which seemed suddenly relevant.

'In Westfield, there was a man who got fired from the railroad for pilfering,' he told Steele.

'What man?'

'His name was—' Colin Babbit battled with his faulty memory. 'Folger,' he said finally. 'Thad Folger was his name.'

'That's it, then,' Steele said with certainty. 'Folger, or someone like him, looted the freight car in Westfield.' He frowned ruefully. Five men dead – all for nothing. Well, he had made worse mistakes, like the time he had ordered the wrong pueblo burned down near Carrizo Gorge, mistakenly believing a rival gang was quartered there. It happened in time of war.

'All right,' Steele said finally. To Waco: 'You boys make yourselves scarce.' To Colin Babbit: 'We obviously don't need the wagon, start back toward Westfield. You might ask around about where this Folger can be found.'

'I'll do that, Mr. Steele,' Babbit said eagerly. He was off the hook with the outlaw leader, it seemed, although he still had to find an explanation to make to the banker. Henry Crimson would not be pleased. Not at all.

Ben Curry had sidled silently up beside Steele and he now spoke in a raw whisper. 'What do you want to do about the witnesses?'

Steele, a hard-boiled outlaw himself was taken aback by the question. 'Do?' he said, looking directly at Frank Ames and a trembling Joe Cox. 'Let them get on with their work, of course. They've a schedule to meet. They didn't see anything.'

Ames, assessing the situation, blurted out, 'No, sir. We couldn't recognize anyone behind those masks you were wearing!'

Curry was standing, hand on his holstered pistol looking wolfish, eager to finish them off, but Steele commanded him, 'You heard the man. We're in the clear.'

'Why would—' Curry persisted, but Steele cut him off.

'Better mount up, Curry. The boys are ready to ride. I'm boss. You've been paid. I don't want to see you around again.'

'You'll be sorry, Steele,' Curry swore.

'Maybe so. I'm sorry about a lot of things,' Trevor Steele said. 'One of them is taking on a man like you.' He turned back to the train men. 'You boys will be late. You've got water in your boiler, you'd better make some track time. Sorry you had that Indian trouble.'

Colin Babbit watched with relief as Curry kind of loped away, like a coyote, he thought. He turned to return to his wagon, but Steele warned him before he clambered aboard, 'You help me find this Thad Folger or else you and I will have a problem. And you don't want to have a problem with me, Babbit.'

Major Richard Fain stood with his hands behind his back, gazing out the window of his office at Fort Thomas, watching the men at mounted drill. They seemed to be doing well enough for what was mostly a group of raw recruits. The glare of the rising sun above the ragged row of hills beyond the fort was brilliant at this early hour, although the parade ground itself lingered in shadow. There was a polite tap at his office door and Fain turned as Lt. Calhoun entered. Young, freshly shaven, his uniform spotless, the second lieutenant had a questioning look in his pale blue eyes.

'Good morning, Mark,' Major Fain said familiarly.

'Good morning, sir,' Mark Calhoun said a little stiffly, as if he half-expected a dressing down from his superior.

'Sit down. Relax,' Fain said with a gesture. 'Have you civilian clothes with you?' he asked unexpectedly.

'Why, yes, sir,' Calhoun replied. What had he been summoned here for?

The major perched on the corner of his desk and smiled, his silver mustache twitching. 'I know you must be puzzled about my summons so early on a work day, Mark, but something has come up.'

'Yes, sir?'

'It is my intention to dispatch you on an detached mission.' Meaning, that it was not battle-related. The major settled himself and got into details. 'As I'm sure you have heard, we were to start receiving shipments of the new Winchester model '73s. We can use those rifles, Mark. They have improved accuracy and firepower over the Springfields. And, I think our men might get a boost in morale, just having the lever-actions handy.

'The problem is,' Fain said with a smile which did not reach his eyes, 'the first shipment has been hijacked somewhere along the train line. And if they've done it once, they can do it again when the next shipment is due. We can't have that. I want you to find these men, whoever they are, and put an end to it.'

Mark Calhoun blinked into the sunlight now streaming through the window. Just how was he supposed to accomplish this?

'I know it's a difficult task, but it is critical. If we have wild Indians or a band of border raiders running around out there with model '73s, even the army won't be able to do much about them should we encounter them.'

'I can see that, sir, but—'

'I know,' Fain said. 'It's asking a lot. I don't know how you will go about things – you'll have to give it a lot of thought and then hope for the best.'

'Of course I'll do my best, sir, but—'

'I'm sending Killeen with you,' the major announced, naming the one man Mark Calhoun detested above all others on the post. Nate Killeen was a civilian scout who had interfered with Calhoun's directives during an engagement with some reservation jumping White Mountain Apaches.

'Sir, Killeen and I—'

'I know you two don't get along,' Fain said, waving a hand. 'But this is for the good of the service. I can't let personal differences influence my decision.'

'But, sir—' Mark began again, realizing he had not been allowed to finish a sentence objecting to matters since he had entered. The reason for that was obvious. Major Fain had his mind firmly set on his course of action. He was simply informing Calhoun of how things must be done, not discussing a strategy.

'You don't have to be friends with the man to get the job done, Lieutenant. You can't tell me that you're fond of every man in your unit.'

'No, sir. Corporal Donahue, for example has the

disgusting habit of—'

'Exactly my point,' Fain said rising to stare out at the parade ground where the men were now being dismissed. With his back to Mark Calhoun, he asked: 'How long have you been out here, Calhoun?'

'Fourteen months now, sir. I was—'

'Exactly,' Fain said as if his point had been made. 'Killeen is an old desert rat. He was here when a white face was a rarity. He knows the Indians and their ways, he knows the back trails and canyons. Lord knows where this quest may lead you. I'd like you to have Killeen along. If he agrees to go,' Fain said with a note of doubt creeping into his voice. After all, Killeen was a civilian employee and could not be ordered to take on the assignment.

'That's about it,' Fain said. 'I can't give you a lot of information about the raid, though it seems from the evidence that they were white. A few bodies were found. The train did get through last night, so maybe you could talk to the crew – what's left of them. It happened down at Comanche Wells, if I neglected to mention that. It's about half way between us and a town called Westfield. Do you know either? It seems a good bet that our raiders are based in Westfield.'

'I know Westfield,' Mark said with his heart rising

a little. That was where he had first met Marie. They were now engaged, or at least had an understanding. He would be able to see her if the investigation took him that far! 'I haven't heard of Comanche Wells, I suppose—'

'There you have it!' Fain said, interrupting again. 'That is why Killeen is going along, you see? He knows every tiny out-of-the-way place strewn across that damnable desert. Now, Mark, change into civilian clothes and pick yourself out a good horse.'

'I have my own mount, sir,' Mark answered, rising from his chair.

'What? Oh, of course, of course,' the major replied. Officers who could afford it usually had their own horses unlike the enlisted men who were required to ride uniformly-colored army bays.

Mark started toward the door, paused to salute and have it returned and heard Fain say, 'Good luck, Mark,' before the door was closed behind him.

In the orderly room Calhoun passed Nate Killeen who was sitting on the bench opposite First Sergeant Duffy's desk. He was dressed in a deep red shell shirt and black jeans. His hat was resting on a crossed knee. Major Fain had described Killeen as an old desert rat, but the scout was not old in years. Perhaps thirty-five, his face desert-tanned, he had slightly curling dark hair worn just-long, cold gray eyes and good teeth which he flashed now as he said, 'Good morning, Lieutenant.'

'Good morning, Killeen,' Calhoun said, forcing out the answer. When he went out, Mark noticed that Killeen was still smiling and that the door to the major's office had opened again to admit him.

This was going to be a hell of a mission, and a long-long shot. Calhoun couldn't see himself succeeding. There was little to go on. But he would find a way to see Marie and that brightened his outlook. Even if he had to trail with that Indian-loving Nate Killeen.

FOUR

'Well,' Tombstone Jack asked miserably, not for the first time, 'we got 'em, now what are we going to do with 'em?' He was referring, of course, to the new Winchester rifles. Tombstone was sitting on a stack of burlap sacking inside Thad Folger's warehouse, watching as Folger finished cleaning the cosmoline off one of the stolen rifles, using a rag dampened with kerosene.

'Isn't that a beautiful piece of work?' Folger asked, admiring the weapon.

'A piece of art,' Tombstone replied solemnly. 'But I was asking what we were going to do with them – like a stolen piece of art, you have to find a market.'

'Why, we'll—' Folger began and then his voice faltered. What were they to do with the rifles?

Everyone on the plains would soon know that an army shipment had gone missing. The weapons were still new, not in wide distribution. Local merchants would not be willing to buy them, certainly not at market price. They could hide the Winchesters away, of course, but by the time these weapons had been forgotten, the model '73s would have flooded the plains, their value plummeting. Even if it could be considered – and Folger had not sunken that low yet – the Indians could not afford to buy them.

Where?

'Maybe we could say we found them and offer to sell them back to the army,' Tombstone suggested hopefully.

'Why would they buy their own arms back from us?' Thad Folger asked. 'Besides, they would never give us more than a finder's fee. Pennies on the dollar.' It was a real dilemma. Folger paced the floor of the musty-smelling barn, searching mentally for an answer. This was the biggest score he had ever made in his pilfering from the railroad – potentially. That word was the stumbling block. Potentially they had a small fortune sitting in those crates, but if they could not sell them they were just a pile of scrap metal.

'There has to be a way,' Jack said.

'Oh, maybe we could do it one rifle at a time, finding buyers on the street, but that seems a very risky way to go about business, Jack.'

'Well, then,' Tombstone Jack said rising from the pile of sacking to stretch. 'I'll leave the thinking to you, Thad. I've still got my job at the depot to see to. But whatever you decide to do, I think it had better be quick. I believe that someone is going to come looking for those weapons, and pretty soon.'

'I think you're right about that, Jack,' Thad Folger answered miserably. They would have to move the rifles soon. But where! How? Thad was completely dejected as Tombstone went out the door of the old barn. There was nothing like sitting on potential wealth and being unable to spend any of it. He let various solutions ramble through his mind until the night's efforts fell on his head like a truncheon and he staggered off to his cot and fell into a disordered slumber.

Someone was bound to come looking. They had pulled off the perfect, imperfect crime.

'What'd they tell you?' Killeen asked. Lieutenant Mark Calhoun rode beside him as they trailed out across the sun-bright desert toward Comanche Wells. Calhoun's horse was a tall white animal with a gray mane and tail; Killeen's was an unremarkable, somewhat shaggy dun he had ridden for years up mountains, across wastelands, and it had always served him well even if it was not pretty. The hammer-headed dun was not always eager to run, but it always served over the long course, though it would never win a prize at a racetrack or beauty contest.

'Well, the train was ready to pull out just as I arrived to interview them,' Calhoun replied. 'I got a few jumbled responses, half of which I was sure were lies. The engineer, Frank Ames, said it was Indians who did it. Joe Cox, the fireman, said that they were masked men.'

'Meaning that they had a good idea who it was, but weren't speaking up out of fear,' Killeen said.

'That was my thought exactly. Have you an idea, Killeen?' Mark asked hopefully.

'A few. Since I think we can throw out the Indian raiders as a concept altogether, it had to be a band of men – criminals – who have use for that many rifles. You should be thinking first about these border gangs – Alberto Mingo's bunch especially.'

'Why him?'

'He's located nearest and his bunch has been the most active lately,' Killeen said with a shrug. 'He's got forty or fifty riders. They raid the small towns up here and then flee to Mexico. If they start their raiding down there and the *federales* get after them, they ride north again.'

'Forty or fifty,' Mark Calhoun said, seemingly stunned. 'What could we do against them?'

'Nothing,' Killeen answered. 'Run is all I can think of. Hell, I doubt the entire Fort Thomas contingent could take Mingo head on – especially if he's got those new rifles.'

They rode on in silence. Comanche Wells was half a day ahead and, Mark Calhoun realized, Marie and Westfield were only another half day's ride away. He brightened a little. He had once observed the young woman as she swam in a pond beneath a stand of sycamore trees. Mark did not think that he was perverted in any way, but the memory of her long, slender legs had been in his mind forever since, hauntingly.

Comanche Wells when they reached it at midday beneath a high-riding white sun, was not a pleasant sight. No one had been there to clean up, and of course the railroad had not had the time to dispatch a new crew to the remote station. They found the station master, McCoy, on his face on the boardwalk before the station, flies and other insects at his flesh. Beneath the water tower they found a young man, Spanish or half-Spanish by his looks, in an equally sickening state of decomposition. Beside the railroad tracks they discovered the body of the brakeman, Walter Cannon, though neither of them knew his name. That was one of the tragedies of war – not even possessing a name to be remembered by. Behind the depot and beside it were two more dead men – raiders apparently.

'We aren't going to learn much here,' Mark Calhoun said to Killeen. 'What are we to do?'

'Bury them, I guess. There isn't much more to be accomplished. Bury them as someone is going to do for us one day.'

Trevor Steele was not happy. He watched the roulette wheel in the Starshine Saloon spin as if mesmerized by it, but his mind was somewhere else. Specifically it was on the profit which he had as yet failed to accrue despite the death of five men in his desert raid. He had sent Colin Babbit off to search for the supposed thief, Thad Folger, but Steele was starting to get the idea that he would never see the coward, Babbit again. *That's what you get for working with amateurs,* he was thinking. No matter; Mingo would have his rifles and Steele would have enough money to continue his preferred lifestyle. He placed his last ten-dollar gold piece down on 'red' as the roulette wheel spun.

*

Marie Slattery sat in her upstairs bedroom looking out across the desert as the rising breeze shifted the light curtains. She knew he was coming. How, she could not have said, but she knew her love was returning to her. Mark Calhoun would be there and they could proceed with their lives as nature intended, living as man and wife. Her father, of course, objected, stating openly and frequently that he did not want his daughter married to a man with such an uncertain and dangerous occupation. The fact that his own job as town marshal could be equally dangerous didn't enter into Slattery's equation. In his own mind he was settled – in fact had one of the nicest homes in Westfield – and his own future was determined, not like some young army officer moving across the plains from outpost to outpost chasing renegade Indians. Now that was a precarious position and one into which he was not willing to allow his young daughter to venture. Harold Slattery was the sort of man who was firmly convinced of his own course and opposed to one he would not have chosen himself.

Once when Marie had told her father that his job was equally dangerous he had leaned back at the dinner table and patted his ample belly, saying 'look at me – I think I've even put on twenty pounds since I took over the job of town marshal.' In fact it was much more than that. 'I take care of my duties, but I don't go racing across the desert chasing Indians!'

Marie doubted that her father was capable of such extended exertion. It did not matter – all she knew was that she was crazy in love with her man, Lieutenant Mark Calhoun, and if one day he were to ask her to ride away with him into the wild country, she would certainly go.

Ben Curry was brooding as he stood at the bar in the Starshine Saloon, watching Trevor Steele at the roulette wheel. The gambler had a fair-sized stack of chips in front of him now and he occasionally passed one off to the blonde hostess with adoring eyes and large breasts. Curry did not like Steele.

Of course he had been paid in advance for his work at the Comanche Wells hold-up, but he had expected a further pay-off once the rifles were found. And if Steele did not want to cut him in, Curry had figured he could make his own plans to sell them to Mingo. Curry had been trying to work his way up in the border gang's hierarchy for quite some time, maybe eventually displacing Mingo who, it was said, was pocketing five thousand a month from his band's depredations. Curry figured he could do with such an income.

Now as he sipped his whiskey, his eyes continued

to stay focused on Trevor Steele in his pressed gray town suit, crafty smile on his face. No wonder Mingo had thrown the man out of the gang. That, of course, was not the way things had happened. Steele had groomed Mingo for years to take his place among the border raiders when he retired, but Curry did not know that. He viewed Steele as weak and incompetent.

For example, the business with the two witnesses at Comanche Wells. Mingo would have silenced them with a bullet; Steele let these men who could identify all of them go free.

That was not Curry's main objection to Steele's way of doing business. He had the idea that Steele knew where the rifles had gotten to and had decided to cut out the men who had been working with him. There was nothing to do for the moment, Curry supposed, but to keep an eye on Steele, to walk in his shadow as it were until the missing '73s could be located.

Steele, playing 'evens', won another fifty dollars as the ball dropped into the twelve slot of the roulette wheel. Curry cursed him. Something had to be done, and obviously Steele wasn't the man to do it. Curry decided to take matters into his own hands.

*

'Well, what is it, man?' Henry Crimson demanded as Colin Babbit showed up unexpectedly at his front door.

'Have to talk,' Colin said, brushing at his long reddish mustache with his fingertips. The banker looked annoyed and petrified with fear at the same time. He had staked all on Babbit's plan.

'Didn't it work?' Crimson asked, stepping out and closing the door behind him. Inside his wife could be heard playing a harpsichord and singing in a faltering soprano voice.

'No, sir, the goods weren't on the train,' Babbit said, glancing at the door which was half-glassed and decorated with sheer white curtains. Crimson was twitching with rage.

'You assured me—'

'I assured you going on the best information I had,' Babbit answered, a little testy now himself. The banker had no right to snap at him. 'I requested, but did not force you to finance the operation.'

'No, no,' Crimson said, running a smoothing hand across his glistening pomaded hair. 'I went into this with my eyes wide open. Have you any ideas?'

'There are five or six stops between Tamarind Springs and Fort Thomas. Obviously we can't look around at all of them. But the seal on the car was obviously broken and we have had a lot of pilferage right here in Westfield by a man known as Folger. I believe he was fired by the Arizona & Eastern for that. It's a good place to start looking.'

'I suppose so,' Crimson said unhappily. 'Can you do that for us, Colin?'

'I guess I'd better,' Babbit replied. 'There will be a lot of folks looking soon – the army, railroad detectives, and I suppose whoever it was that wanted to steal the Winchesters in the first place.'

Crimson grew intent as his wife segued into another badly played song within the house. 'Try! It's ruin for me if we can't find those rifles!'

Colin Babbit, who had his suspicions about Thad Folger, found the man's hideout without great difficulty. Westfield was a small town. Little happened that wasn't observed. Being told by neighboring farmers that Folger had rented the disused barn from a man named Paulsen, someone whom Babbit had never met, and had been observed frequently driving a wagon into the barn, Babbit made his decision. Folger was a well-known pilferer, had in fact been fired for his thieving habits by the railroad. Only Marshal Slattery seemed unaware of his goings-on, but then Slattery seemed unaware of almost everything in his own town. Or was supremely indifferent to it all.

At any rate, under a three-quarter midnight moon, Colin Babbit rode on toward the old barn, convinced in his own mind that it was Thad Folger who was behind the theft of the Winchester '73s.

And Colin needed to retrieve them – the banker, Henry Crimson, was out a lot of money. Trevor Steele was feeling defeated. Both men placed the failure of the enterprise squarely on Babbit's shoulders. Colin had to redeem himself. Besides, he thought, as he passed through the oak grove surrounding the barn, plunging himself into murky moon-shadows, he was broke himself and desperately needed the cash just to survive. He had few resources. Long ago he had been the foreman at a prosperous cattle ranch but he had let himself be caught affixing his own brand to maverick steers and dismissed; his hope for a rich beginning ended. Since then he had become a roamer, taking opportunity where he found it. He sometimes thought that his old saddle partner, Pierce Avery, had been the smarter when he took that office job with the railroad, but Colin Babbit had been much younger then and young men are seldom able to look far down the road.

'Hell,' he grumbled to himself as he rode on,

there had even been a time when he had a sharing woman; although she was little rounder than most men prefer, she had liked him well enough, even done his cooking and laundry before he had been forced to make his escape from the west Texas lands after the branding incident. What did he have now? A fifty-dollar horse and two silver dollars in his pocket.

The barn loomed large and dark before Colin. There was no sign of activity within, although Colin Babbit had cut the signs of recent wagon traffic along the way. A heavy wagon. He was sure he was on the right scent. He drew his Colt revolver from his holster and walked his horse nearer, his eyes cautiously searching the surrounding area. Nothing moved; there was no sound to be heard but the singing of the light breeze in the high reaches of the lonesome oaks.

Ten yards from the barn Babbit swung down from his pony and eased his way closer to the barn. He eyed the twin front doors, judged them to be faultily hung on rusty, creaking hinges and worked his way around the structure, seeking a side entrance.

Finding the narrow door at the rear of the barn he took a slow breath and entered the horse-smelling building in three rapid steps. Nothing moved; no one challenged his entry. He crouched and let his eyes adjust to the darkness. As they slowly did, he saw a few scattered crates and boxes, saw the figure of what appeared to be a sleeping man in the corner, lying on a cot. He went that way, his pistol cocked and ready to fire.

At the foot of the bed stood the unmistakable form of a Winchester rifle. Babbit smiled against the darkness and crept nearer.

He was small steps away from his goal when one of the huge front barn doors was swung wide on complaining hinges, and a man with a gun appeared. Babbit switched his own sights that way and was met with immediate gunfire. He was not able to recognize the border raider, Ben Curry, as he returned the fire. Babbit's legs sagged underneath him and his gun was flung away by a last reflex, but not before he had let loose two .44 caliber rounds which slammed into Curry's body, hastily aimed though they had been. The first had broken Curry's knee cap and, as he had sagged away, the second, almost fired inadvertently, had drilled him through the forehead as he slumped downward.

Thad Folger was jerked into consciousness by the racketing of the close gunfire in the barn. He searched frantically for his own pistol, could not find it, and discovered as his sleep cleared that it did not matter. There were two dead men there, lying against the barn floor as the smoke from their weapons cleared away.

Thad's heart was racing. He had figured on this, or something like it happening. He was beginning to regret his life of petty crime. He felt like abandoning the spoils of his theft, dismissed the idea and quickly got dressed. He had to find Tombstone Jack. They needed to load up a wagon and get out of there! Quickly. He did not recognize either of the two men in the barn by lantern light, but he knew one thing – they would not be the last to come looking for those stolen repeating rifles.

FIVE

Tombstone Jack wasn't exactly drunk, but no one would have called him sober either. He spent long hours at the depot watching for late trains, sweeping up a little, and the nights grew tiresome and boring. Whiskey helped him smooth the way across his long shifts. He wasn't expecting to see Thad Folger again so soon.

'What's up?' Tombstone asked, as Thad Folger reined up on the stocky roan horse he had purchased only that day.

'Oh, nothing,' Thad said, obviously untruthfully. He swung down from his horse, looked around at the darkened depot and asked, 'Are you busy tonight?'

'No more than usual,' Tombstone Jack replied, taking a sip from his steel whiskey flask. 'Why do you ask?'

'Because we have some work to do, Jack,' Thad Folger said, crouching in front of Jack.

'What kind of work?' Jack asked uneasily.

'We've got to move those rifles. Some men figured out that we had them. Two of them came to the barn tonight and well – they shot each other dead.'

Jack eyed Folger closely. 'You're not lying, are you, Thad? Well, damn all! I knew I didn't want to get tangled up with you and your talk of predation! Murder, you say? What can we do about it? The marshal will have to get involved in this now, and we're stuck in the middle of it.'

'I know that, Jack; that's what I'm saying – we have to move those guns and do it fast!' Folger said earnestly. 'Otherwise all of this will have been for nothing.'

'As far as I can see, it has all been for nothing anyway,' Jack said sourly. 'Unless you have come up with an idea of how to sell those rifles.'

'Jack,' Folger pleaded, 'you have got to help me. Otherwise our backs are up against the wall. Even Marshal Slattery will be able to figure it out and we'll be doing hard time in a federal prison.'

'I am still a working man,' Tombstone protested as if that put him a notch above Thad Folger. 'I'm not supposed to leave my post.'

'Oh, hell, Jack, you're not supposed to do a lot of things,' he said, indicating the whiskey flask with a nod of his head. 'But it won't take long and Quentin Garrett is home snoring by now with his nose up his wife's fat ass.'

'That's kind of crude,' Tombstone said.

'I have a vivid imagination,' Folger said. 'And a lack of respect for preda—'

'Don't say it again,' Jack urged, showing both palms to Folger. 'I'll go along with you. I guess I have to – so long as I never hear that word again. It's what started all of this, if you don't recall.'

Wally Shoup, the owner of the Trail's End Stable was not happy to be awakened at this late hour by Tombstone, but it was a part of his business. Long-riding men arrived at all hours, looking to board their horses. What was unusual was a local man wanting to rent a wagon for the second time in the same day. 'Aren't you supposed to be working?' Shoup asked, sleepily scratching his head.

'I am,' Jack said, offering his hastily concocted story. 'Garrett wants me to move some freight around while things are quiet.'

'Oh, well,' Shoup muttered, neither believing nor disbelieving the tale. His job was to make a few dollars out of the feeding and sheltering of horses and the rental of buggies and wagons, not to concern himself with some railroad boss's strange ideas. 'I can give you the same wagon and team, Tombstone. Those horses seemed little used. You should see the condition some of them are in when they're returned! Like the team Babbit hired. . . .'

'Let's just take care of business,' Jack said. No one ever wanted to listen to the stable owner's stories.

Well, the men were dead all right. On closer examination, Jack and Thad Folger recognized Colin Babbit from around town. The second man seemed vaguely familiar, but they could not put a name to him.

Like many others, Ben Curry would go to his unmarked grave unremembered and unidentified.

There was a lingering feeling in both Tombstone Jack's and Folger's minds that these would not be the last of the men to die for the stolen rifles.

The crates containing the Winchesters were loaded on to the wagon, although Folger thought he could get away with concealing the rest of the stolen property and had already thought up half a dozen excuses for having the merchandise around – he could come up with none for having the model '73s, and so with midnight turning the date they drove eastward along the gravel road beside Lodi Creek, the two dead men and the rifles in the wagon bed.

Folger had the one Winchester that he had stripped of its cosmoline coating between his knees on the wagon seat, and Jack asked, 'Do you think it's a good idea to carry that thing around?'

'Who knows,' Folger shot back. 'But I think we may get into some trouble. Is there something you'd rather have for protection?'

'I guess not,' Jack said. He was growing more morose as the night shifted past.

'What are we going to do with the cargo, Folger?' Jack asked after an hour beneath the high-riding moon.

'Those two back there,' Thad Folger said without passion, 'I suppose we can cut them loose to drift downriver. The rifles – I have in mind dropping them into an old mine shaft I know of. We'll tie ropes around the crates so that they can be brought back up quickly after I contact the people I have in mind.'

'What people?' Tombstone Jack asked. Folger hadn't mentioned any purchaser by name.

'You'll find out . . . at the right time,' Folger replied, and Tombstone wondered if Folger wasn't inventing a solution to their problem. Neither had so far seen a cent of profit, and their prospects were dimming. Jack thought as he guided the two-horse team onward in the night, that he may now have lost his real job, his only job, already by falling in with Folger. If Garrett ever found out that he had left his post at the depot on this night, he would certainly be fired. Oh, a man could be such a fool. Tombstone found himself wishing that he was at home on this night with his nose in some fat woman's ass.

It could be a confusing world with little comfort to be found.

They bid farewell to the dead men – Colin Babbit and the other man whom they could not identify – a mile farther on. It may have been more Christian to bury them, but it was certainly swifter to throw them into the quick-running Lodi Creek and mentally wave goodbye as they drifted their way toward Mexico.

The rifles were next.

They hauled them on another mile or so until Thad Folger indicated a side track which climbed into the rocky hills covered with sage brush and thickly growing manzanita. Tombstone looked at the suggested trail dubiously.

'I spent a summer working up there, Tombstone. It leads to the Old Crazy Eights Mine if you remember it. They never took much ore out of it, but they dug a lot of holes which suit our purpose.'

Still doubtful, Tombstone Jack started the reluctant team up the washed-out, rocky trail. The moon was already sagging low in the west by the time they reached the old mining camp which had two tumbledown structures still standing.

'I'm trying to remember,' Folger said. Finally he pointed to their right and Tombstone guided the horses that way. 'It's been a long time,' Folger felt obliged to say in his defense, 'and everything is different in the darkness.'

'Just find us a hole,' Jack said wearily. The entire episode was starting to seem like madness now. He wasn't sure if he actually even cared about the job any more. He continued only because he had given his word to Thad, and for fear that he would return to the Westfield Station to find Quentin Garrett waiting to fire him.

It was long after midnight and the crates seemed heavier than ever as they lowered them from the wagon bed and fitted them with cradles of rope, lowered them down into a mine shaft of unknown depth and backed away from the toil, perspiring heavily. The exposed ropes had to be covered with narrow cairns of concealing rock. By the time that was done Tombstone Jack, no longer a young man, had had it with this night's work.

So apparently had Folger who leaned up against

the wagon, mopping at his brow with a blue bandanna. Yet Folger managed a smile and told Jack, 'That's over. Now all we have to do is wait for payday.'

'When do you figure that might be?' Jack drawled.

'You see, Jack,' Folger said, clambering up on to the wagon as the darkness grew heavier and a light breeze began to rise, lifting dust around them, 'I've told you that I have a lot of contacts. I met a man who knows a man who can get rid of the rifles for us and see that we make a good profit. In the meantime,' he shrugged, as Tombstone started the team homeward with a snap of the reins across their flanks, 'if you need a little money to get by on, I can let you have some as soon as tomorrow. I can unload the bolts of cloth, the clocks and those panes of glass pretty easily.'

'Well, if I have a need,' Jack answered, 'I'll ask,' as he stepped on the wagon's high brake to slow the wagon on the grade. What was Folger figuring on – handing over five or ten dollars? After all of this!

In fact Thad Folger *had* met a man who knew a man. He was a thin blond character who called himself Waco and during a round of drinking at the Starlight Saloon, Folger had finally brought the subject up as a hypothetical question. Waco had been interested; very interested.

The man Waco knew was Trevor Steele who still desperately wanted those Winchesters, the raid on Comanche Wells having netted him nothing. To make matters more urgent Steele had encountered another of the former border raiders, a man named Blake and forgotten himself and bragged that he was about to come into possession of thirty to fifty of the model '73s, and advised Blake to tell Mingo to have the cash ready for a purchase if he wanted first claim on them.

To Steele, despite his recent run of luck at the roulette table, this was a make or break operation. The recent raid on the railroad station only served to solidify in his own mind that he was better suited at this time of life to the profession of gentleman gambler than returning to the wild ways.

Waco's news was buoying to Steele, though Waco could offer few details about the location and price of the rifles. No matter, the details would be taken care of in time. Trevor Steele just knew that he had the chance to make one big score before retiring from crime forever. His luck had finally turned on all fronts.

Of course Steele knew that Mingo would come to Westfield himself to take care of business and knew as well that he did not want to disappoint Mingo.

The few men who had done that were planted across the lonesome desert in unmarked graves. Old friendships, old loyalties meant little among the border raiders.

'It won't look good on my record if we can't solve this,' Lieutenant Mark Calhoun commented as they rode across the long plain, approaching Westfield in the near dawn hours.

'I guess not,' Killeen said. He had removed both lanky legs from the stirrups to stretch them briefly. 'But it's a tough assignment.'

'A capable officer completes difficult assignments,' Calhoun said in a pontificating tone.

'That sounds good,' Killeen answered, 'but difficult things are always . . . difficult.'

'You don't really care, do you, Killeen?' an obviously miffed Calhoun demanded. 'You can ride away from the army and it wouldn't mean much to you.'

'Not a lot,' Killeen admitted. 'It's good enough work, scouting for the cavalry – it sure beats spending days and nights staring at the back ends of steers on a cattle drive, but it is not a be-all and end-all to me, you're right about that.' Killeen winked in the near-darkness. 'But, Lieutenant Calhoun, I take pride in always finishing what I have started.'

'Maybe you can find out something by hanging around the railroad depot,' Lieutenant Calhoun suggested to Killeen as they approached Westfield, squinting into the glare of the harsh morning sunlight, hats tugged low to protect their eyes. Calhoun was now wearing a pearl-buttoned white shirt and tan twill trousers. For some reason – perhaps because he had no others – he had continued to wear his regulation cavalry boots, but this was not something that would inspire speculation in a country where at least half the adult male population had been servicemen at some point in their lives.

'I'd be willing to try that after we stable up the horses,' Killeen answered. 'What are you going to be doing?'

'I thought I should talk with the town marshal,' Calhoun said easily, neglecting to mention that Marie was Marshal Slattery's daughter.

'That might be helpful,' Killeen had to admit. 'Where's his office in case I come up with something?'

'Right up the street on the left,' Calhoun said waving an indifferent hand. 'It's still too early for him to be in. I know where his house is. I'm riding out there.'

'All right,' Killeen said, with a hint of suspicion.

What was the young officer up to? He was obviously concealing something. 'I'm going to put my horse up then, and walk over to the depot.'

Again raising a negligent hand, Mark Calhoun started his pony out of town into the face of the rising sun, running it at a faster pace than the trail-beaten white horse would have liked.

'Man's in a hurry,' Killeen muttered to himself and then gave up speculating on the young officer's motives. Killeen swung down from his weary dun where he had halted and took the animal's reins, leading it toward the nearest stable. Wally Shoup emerged from the back office scratching at his belly and squinting into the blinding light of early morning. He looked worn down as if he hadn't slept at all.

Killeen commented on it. 'Have a rough night of it?' he asked Shoup.

'You could say so,' Shoup answered, taking the dun's reins from Killeen. 'Everybody wanting wagons in the middle of the night. They keep the team and wagon out all night, then come back to wake me up again before dawn. . . .'

'Just see that my dun is watered, grained, rubbed down and curried a little,' Killeen said, interrupting Shoup. The stableman had expected as much – no one ever listened to his stories.

'What's the quickest way to walk to the railroad depot?' Killeen inquired.

Shoup gave instructions, thought again about trying his tale of the railroad worker over there wanting the wagon in the middle of the night and gave it up as a bad idea. Killeen had already turned his back, was already walking away as Shoup led the dun to a rear stall to unsaddle it.

'As I was saying,' Shoup said to the dun as he undid the cinches on its saddle. He had pretty much given up on men listening to his stories although the horses did not seem to mind a bit and he had formed the habit of telling them about his tribulations. 'When Tombstone came back in with that team, it was already close to dawn. . . .'

The dun horse listened with interest. It had been a long while since he had heard a good story.

There were half a dozen people waiting on the station platform when Killeen arrived at the train station: an old woman in black sitting hunched on a wooden bench, a younger woman in yellow nervously looking up the tracks, a man with a woman in blue, obviously his wife, with two young towheaded kids tugging at her skirts for attention. It was pretty obvious that they were all expecting a train, and from the direction they were watching, it was an eastbound passenger train they were waiting for. People going home? People going to a funeral? People going to get married or meet a loved one? They all had their stories; Killeen didn't bother trying to sort out the possibilities.

He was more interested in some specific missing freight.

The obvious place to start was in the office of the depot and Killeen started that way, guided by a small red arrow painted on a sign. Frowning, he approached the door to find it closed and locked. It was still early.

'Looking for somebody?' called out a youngish man peering out of a small arched window carved into the face of the building.

'Whoever's in charge,' Killeen said to the man who was obviously a ticket clerk.

'That's Quentin Garrett. You won't have to wait long,' said the young man looking at a large railroad watch. 'Mr. Garrett is on a schedule as regular as our trains. He'll be arriving in fifteen minutes.'

'All right. Thank you,' Killeen said. He thought he had just been given a learned speech on the efficiency of the railroad, but it didn't bother him. He had fifteen minutes to spare although his stomach was starting to complain of his lack of attention to its needs. Seeing no place else to sit, he lowered himself on to the far end of the bench where the woman in black sat dabbing at her eyes with a handkerchief. Yes, there was something wrong in her world. The children had given up on capturing their mother's attention and decided to race up and down the platform, screaming loudly. The pretty younger woman in yellow still stared hopefully into the distances. For her man? Killeen supposed there were a lot of little dramas underway anywhere that traveling people congregated.

Without warning a man lurched out of the shadows, stumbled across the platform, narrowly missing the little girl and pitched face-first on to the steel rails below.

Tombstone Jack had found his limit of whiskey.

SIX

The two younger women shrieked. The old lady in black began crying again as Jack tumbled from the platform. The two children started dancing and pointing as if Jack had performed a clever trick for their amusement. The father of the unruly kids muttered something that sounded like, 'For God's sake!' at his wife but remained fixed where he was. Killeen vaulted off the platform, spurred on by the whistle, grumble and clank of an arriving locomotive, now not that far away, racing along the tracks toward them.

Kneeling beside Tombstone between the rails, Killeen lifted the man's head and said, 'Come on, old-timer. There's a train coming.'

Tombstone didn't move. There was a lump on the side of his head the size of a hen's egg and his eyes were unfocused. Killeen glanced up, expecting some help, at least from the young husband, but he got none. They all stood nearly in a row, simply staring down at him, the children clapping their hands.

Muttering a seldom-used, almost forgotten curse, Killeen reached down and scooped Tombstone up in his arms as the locomotive bore down on them, its brakes screeching, its whistle shrilling. There was no easy way up and over the lip of the depot platform, so Killeen chose to carry Tombstone across the tracks and deposit him in the unkempt brush there just before the iron behemoth clanked to a stop at the Westfield Station. A man peered out at Killeen.

'Is he all right?' Frank Ames, the engineer, called out above the whoosh of escaping steam.

'I think so!' Killeen shouted back.

'I saw you, but these things don't stop on a dime, you know!'

'It's all right. It's not your fault,' Killeen answered, his heart still pounding. He returned his attention to the stunned Tombstone Jack.

Crouching down again, Killeen again looked around, expecting some help, but none came. He lifted Tombstone's head and placed it on his lap and finally Jack's eyes flickered open. He gazed dumbly at Killeen.

'Take it easy for a minute,' Killeen said. 'We'll get you fixed up. What happened, anyway?'

'I am a man at the mercy of hard liquor,' Jack muttered. At least that was what it sounded like he said. His voice was incredibly slurred.

'It's all right. We'll find you a cot or at least a comfortable place to lie down. You'll be all right.'

Jack coughed once, twice. Then he clutched at Killeen's shirt sleeve with a claw-like hand and added quite distinctly:

'Mister, take my advice. Don't ever get tangled up with no predators!'

'No,' Killeen said in a soft voice though he had no idea in the world what Jack was talking about. It would take the man awhile to get over that crack on the head – or the alcohol – both of which were contributing to causing this confusion in his mind.

Killeen waited on the side of the tracks until the train was once more ready to roll and with an ear-piercing shriek of its whistle and the clanging of its bell, the grinding of the heavy iron drive wheels searching for purchase, it finally churned away from the station.

'What's all this!' a voice from the platform demanded after the train had pulled out. Killeen looked up to see a medium-sized man with thinning black hair swept across a balding dome, wearing gold-rimmed glasses staring down at them.

'This man has been injured. Who are you?'

'The name is Quentin Garrett,' the man answered with a voice filled with self-importance. 'I am the station master here. Jack? Jack, is that you?'

' 'S me,' Jack answered though his voice was too weak to carry far. He grinned stupidly up at Killeen and said 'Ask him about his nose,' which meant nothing to Killeen. Then he fell into cackling laughter which broke off in a fit of coughing.

'What happened to him?' Garrett wanted to know.

'I don't know exactly,' Killeen called back. 'I don't think he's hurt bad, but we'd better get him up out of here and to bed. If I can get some help. . . .'

'All right,' Garrett said with resignation. 'I'll send someone.' He then turned and called out, 'Toby!' and in a minute the young man from the ticket office appeared, frowning at the sight.

Within minutes Killeen and Toby had lugged Tombstone Jack up out of the bushes, carried him across the tracks and up a ramp at the far end of the depot platform to the office. 'He has a little room downtown,' Garrett said, opening the green-painted door, 'but for now I suppose we'd better let him rest on a bed I have in back.' Garrett got a whiff of Tombstone's breath in passing. As was obvious to Killeen, the raw whiskey smell alone was strong enough to strangle a man.

'I should have guessed,' Garrett said as they took Tombstone through an interior door and placed him on a small bed. 'Whiskey. I don't know how many times I've talked to Jack about it.' Garrett rubbed his own face with both hands. 'I should fire him, but he's off-duty now although we both know a man couldn't have gotten that drunk in the hour since he was off the clock.'

'I've seen men do amazing things with liquor,' Killeen said a little protectively. 'Besides the whiskey might not be what caused his fall.'

'I think it was,' Garrett said as if the weight of the world were on his shoulders, 'but I've just recently lost another man, and there aren't many men around who would take on the night-security post.' He said all this almost mournfully.

'Did you ask him?' Tombstone asked from his bed.

'Ask him what?'

'You know,' Jack said snickering stupidly.

'I will,' Killeen answered.

'Do you have any idea what he's talking about?' Garrett asked as they went into his office, closing the door behind them, letting Toby make his way back toward the ticket booth.

'No,' Killeen answered truthfully. 'That knock on his skull seems to have scrambled him up considerably.'

Seating himself behind his low, scarred desk, Garrett looked Killeen in the eyes and asked, 'And you, sir? Just who are you, and what is your business here?'

The morning sun slanted through the only window in the room as Killeen told Garrett what he was doing in Westfield. The station master nodded now and then, understanding the army's position as well as his own. If the railroad couldn't guarantee shipments, the army would find another way to deliver the new weapons to its far-flung posts – cavalry-guarded wagon trains – and that would cost the Arizona & Eastern good money.

'I have a suspect for you,' Garrett said suddenly. His small eyes gleamed behind the lenses of his spectacles. Killeen was willing to listen.

'Who might that be?'

'Not long ago I discovered that a man named Thad Folger was pilfering from the freight shipments that passed through here. Of course I had to let him go.'

'Of course,' Killeen replied, and asked, 'Did –

what's his name, Jack – know Folger well?'

'They were pretty close friends, I'd say. Why do you ask?'

'Well, I'm not a lawman, and I don't know how they go about their investigations, but it seems to me that Jack might have had a reason for getting so tanked up this early in the morning. Something that was worrying him, say.'

'You may have a point,' Garrett said thoughtfully.

'I'd like to stay around and talk to him in a few hours, if I may.'

'Of course!' Garrett said expansively. 'The railroad and I have a stake in this matter as well.'

'Then, after the marshal has been consulted – that is where my partner, Lieutenant Calhoun, is at the moment – we might be able to formulate a reasonable plan of action.'

'Calhoun?' Garrett asked, now standing behind his desk, still blinking into the morning sunlight. 'Surely that's not the young officer who was courting Harold Slattery's daughter.'

'I didn't know Marshal Slattery had a daughter,' Killeen said honestly. But it explained Mark Calhoun's actions. 'I don't suppose that matters much as far as our investigation goes.'

'No,' Garrett said. 'I suppose not.' But his words were doubtful, and they planted a seed of that doubt in Killeen's mind. As the sun lazed its way higher into the pale sky, the weariness of the previous night's long ride translated itself into a need for sleep. Killeen could afford a room in the town's hotel – after all the army was paying for it – but he did not wish to leave Tombstone Jack who was now not only an accident victim but a possible witness to the theft, and might decide to run off. In the end Killeen decided to let Garrett go about his business and he stretched out on the wooden floor beside Jack's bed. It was not comfortable, but Killeen had slept in worse places and under more pressure.

He fell off to sleep with Jack steadily snoring and the sun beaming in through the low window.

Sometime after noon Killeen heard the hooting of another approaching train and he sat up on the floor. Tombstone was already awake, if you could call it that. He was on his back, staring at the ceiling with bleary eyes. He glanced at Killeen and muttered, 'Bad liquor.'

'Good liquor can have that effect too.'

'Can it? I wouldn't know. I never drank any.'

'Can you sit up and talk to me for a minute?' Killeen asked.

'I can talk to you – it's the sitting up part I'm not sure I can manage.'

Killeen introduced himself and told Jack what his

business was. He sat on the edge of Jack's bed. Those bleary eyes of Tombstone's now had begun to show some fear. 'I need to find Thad Folger and talk to him.'

'What about?'

'I think you know what about,' Killeen said. 'I am going to find those rifles sooner or later. It'll be better for you both if you help me to do it sooner.'

'What makes you think I had anything to do with it?' Jack asked, propping himself up on one elbow.

'I didn't say that. I said I wanted to talk to Folger. Come on, Jack, tell me about it. You've still got a job – Garrett told me as much. I'm not here to prosecute anyone; I just want those '73s back. That's all the army wants. You made one mistake; no one's going to hold it against you.'

'I'm continuing to hold it against my own self,' Jack said miserably. 'It's made my life hell.'

'That bad?'

'That bad.'

'Now's the time to crawl out from under the trouble. Just tell me where Folger is, and where the rifles are.'

'You'll never find the rifles,' Jack said. 'Not where we put them.'

'Where's that?'

'Funny thing is I can't remember exactly.' Jack

said, holding his head. 'Down a hole somewhere. I'm telling you the truth. I took a pretty good knock on the skull. It seems to have driven that piece of memory out of my head.'

Killeen got to his feet. He hadn't solved this yet, but he was getting closer. 'You'd better tell me where Folger is, then,' he told Tombstone. 'And keep in mind, refusing to do so will mark you down in my book as uncooperative.'

'I'll tell you where he is, or rather where I last saw him, Killeen. Give me a minute. There's a lot of fog in my head, whirling all around. Let me have a piece of paper off that desk and I'll draw you a map.'

Now Tombstone did manage to sit up and Killeen gave him a pencil and a piece of blank paper. With great difficulty, it seemed, the still-dazed man drew a map of the way to Paulsen's barn. 'He might not be there,' Tombstone said. 'He might have gone off to peddle his bolts of cloth. Or . . . he might have already met up with the men who are going to buy those rifles.

'Who are they?' Killeen asked with some immediacy. Tombstone shook his head heavily.

'He never did get around to telling me that,' Jack answered.

'All right,' Killeen said heavily. 'I guess I'd better

get out and try to find Folger.'

'Don't tell him that I informed on him!' Jack pleaded.

'I can't see any point in that,' Killeen said reassuringly. 'You'd better try to make your way home and try to get some decent sleep.'

'That's what I intended to do,' Jack said. He still looked too shaky to make it to his feet. Killeen had turned to go when Jack asked, 'Mister, could you let me have a few dollars? I don't think I can make it all the way to home without stopping for a few whiskeys.'

Killeen made his way back to the middle of Westfield and began looking up and down the street for Mark Calhoun. Not seeing his distinctive white horse he returned to the stable to check on his own mount.

Where was Calhoun and what was the young officer doing?

From in front of the stable, Wally Shoup watched Killeen approaching along the sun-bright street, his boots kicking up fans of fine yellow dust in his passing. From in front of the Starshine Saloon, Trevor Steele also glanced at the tall man with interest. He wondered about the stranger. But Steele's eyes, narrowed by the glare of the sun, were more concentrated on the far ends of the street where he expected soon to spot the familiar bulky figure of Alberto Mingo arriving in Westfield. Steele still didn't know the location of the rifles, but Waco assured him that he had made contact with the man who was holding them.

Waco was a trustworthy man. He and Steele had ridden the long trails together, and Steele trusted him more than anyone in his group, including the mysterious Tom Bull. It could all be sorted out. The thing was, Steele wanted to have the rifles on hand when Mingo arrived – it gave him a better bargaining position. He needed to find the man who had the '73s and secure them before Mingo arrived, to avoid being cut out of the deal.

Trevor Steele thought he still held the winning hand in this game. All of life was a gamble; anything could go wrong at any moment. But Steele had the nerve to play in high-stakes games. He had done so all of his life.

SEVEN

'It's about time,' Killeen grumbled an hour later as Mark Calhoun returned to Wally Shoup's stable. 'Where in hell have you been?'

'I told you, Killeen,' the army lieutenant answered a little huffily as he swung down from his horse, 'I have been conferring with the marshal.'

'Have you now? I have a good view of the marshal's office from here. Slattery's been there for at least half an hour.'

Calhoun muttered and mumbled without really saying anything as he unsaddled.

Killeen said, 'My pony's rested and I'm ready to ride, Lieutenant. I suppose you'd better rent a mount.'

'Ride where?' Calhoun asked in confusion.

'To find the man with the rifles – I think I know

where he is.' Killeen smiled and shook his head. 'I'll tell you about it along the way. I hope you at least got Marshal Slattery's blessing.'

'For the—?'

'For the wedding, you damned fool! Now find yourself a pony and let's get moving.'

Ten minutes later they were riding the sun-drenched street out of Westfield toward Paulsen's barn – Killeen again in the saddle of his dumpy dun horse, Mark Calhoun riding a leggy sorrel. They had just reached the town limits when a group of incoming riders – five or six men in all – passed them going in the opposite direction. Their leader was a bulky man with a flourishing black mustache wearing a flounced white shirt and dark twill trousers. Killeen thought he recognized the man and quickly turned his head away so that he, himself, would not be recognized.

'That was a tough-looking bunch,' Lieutenant Calhoun said after the men had exchanged dust and continued on their ways.

'Yes. They are,' Killeen answered and Calhoun studied him more deliberately.

'You say that as if you know them.'

'Not all of them, not personally, but they are part of a gang of border raiders. And the man with the big mustache was their leader, Alberto Mingo.'

'You sound pretty sure.'

'I am. A long time ago I was scouting for General Crook when he had a little dust-up with them. We pursued them toward Mexico, but we had to stop at the border. The raiders, of course, kept going.'

'What could they be doing in Westfield?' Mark Calhoun asked, now worried not only about the mission, but about the safety of Marie Slattery.

'I have an idea, and it should have occurred to you as well by now.'

'You don't mean the new Winchesters!'

'I do – think about it. What bigger prize is there for them to try to take around here?'

'We should return and warn the marshal!' Calhoun said, his voice growing a little hectic.

'No. We should find and secure those rifles as soon as possible,' Killeen argued.

'Yes,' Calhoun said, 'of course you're right, Killeen. That is all we can do.'

'We at least have an idea now of who has the model '73s and who they are intended for. That's a lot further ahead then where we were yesterday.'

'All thanks to you,' Lieutenant Calhoun said dismally.

'I fell into some luck – almost literally,' Killeen answered. 'That's all there is to it. Besides it doesn't matter; we're here to work as a team. That's what

Major Fain sent us down here for.'

'Yes,' Mark Calhoun said, nodding, 'but I wonder if he didn't send me down here because I am an army officer, and you to baby-sit me.'

Killeen didn't answer. The young lieutenant was taking things too hard. Maybe he felt that he had neglected his duty by riding to see Marie. Killeen didn't blame him for that; he might have done the same in Mark's position. And it was difficult to see what help Calhoun could have been had he remained in town. As he had told the officer, Killeen had just stumbled upon the right man to point him in the right direction. Now the trick was to find Folger and the cache of weapons before Mingo did.

Killeen didn't like the image he could create in his mind of the havoc thirty of Mingo's savage border raiders armed with the '73s might raise across the territory. As Major Fain had pointed out, even the army would have no chance against a large force of men armed with the new repeaters.

They rode steadily eastward across a land studded with occasional stands of oak trees, the sun glinting in their high reaches, Killeen occasionally consulting the crude map Tombstone Jack had sketched out for him at the depot.

'If only we could—' Mark Calhoun began when

they were suddenly approached by a man driving a surrey toward them. Behind the seat was a canvas tarp covering a pile of goods.

'This could be our man,' Killeen said quietly. Beyond the oaks he had caught sight of a gray, leaning barn.

'Do you think so?'

'I don't know, but we're going to halt him and have a conversation,' Killeen said.

They guided their horses to the center of the road, leaving no room for the surrey to pass by. The driver, obviously irritated at their lack of road courtesy, reined in the roan horse drawing his buggy.

'It's him,' Killeen said, basing his certainty only on a vague description that Tombstone Jack had provided and the fact that the man was pulling away from the disused barn. 'Take charge, Calhoun, you're the officer.'

Calhoun did, resuming or feigning confidence. He took the bridle of the roan horse and said authoritatively: 'So we've finally run you down, Folger!'

'Get out of my way!' Folger shouted. 'Who are you?'

'Lieutenant Mark Calhoun, Fort Thomas. Mister Killeen – examine the property this man is carrying.'

Killeen rode alongside the unhappy Folger's rig – he had not denied his name – and whipped the tarp away from the covered goods in back. Calhoun's triumphant expression fell away as he did; Killeen's own face must have reflected disappointment. What they had found were half a dozen bolts of cloth, some glass panes and six brass-bound clocks, all obviously stolen merchandise, but of no interest to them.

'What are you men looking for?' Folger demanded.

'More of these,' Nate Killeen said coldly, for he had seen sunlight glimmer on the metal of a rifle barrel and he leaned low in the saddle to lift the new Winchester '73 that Thad Folger had taken for his own use from the stolen shipment.

'I can't see—' Folger sputtered, reflecting that Tombstone Jack had been right when he had advised him not to carry the weapon around.

'That seems to be US Army property,' Calhoun said coldly. 'You have a choice – cooperate with us or be hanged.'

'You can't—' Folger began to object before realizing that he had no idea what they could or could not legally do.

'Will you take us to the rest of the weapons?' Killeen said. 'You might as well know that

Tombstone Jack has already confessed.'

'That damned drunk,' they heard Folger mutter.

'Maybe,' Killeen answered. 'But Jack is off the hook now and you're still on it, Folger. Tell us where those rifles are and maybe we can still keep you off the scaffold.'

Folger was silent for a few minutes: greed, his native slyness, sense of self-preservation and panic all circling his mind.

'I'll show you – if you give me a promise in writing not to prosecute,' he finally said. 'You'll need a wagon, though.'

'Lieutenant?' Killeen asked.

'I think we can provide both, on my own authority but God help you, Folger. If you renege, I'll hang you myself!'

Mark Calhoun, Killeen thought, was so fiery because he believed that his career hung in the balance with this mission. He would become either a decorated young officer sure to be promoted for achieving a difficult task or a man disgraced because he had been off wooing a girl when he should have been concentrating on his job. Well, no one but Killeen could know that but as they started back toward Westfield for a wagon, Calhoun's eyes betrayed his mistrust of Killeen.

'Let's start back toward town, then,' Calhoun

said, his primacy restored. 'We're going to need a heavier wagon.'

'Maybe now is the time to let Marshal Slattery in on affairs,' Killeen suggested.

'Yes, it might be,' Calhoun answered as they started back toward Westfield. If all went right this could boost his stock with not only the army but with Marie's father. Temporarily buoyed, Calhoun led the way sitting tall in the saddle of his rented sorrel horse, a dejected Thad Folger following.

'I suppose I owe you for this,' Mark Calhoun said to Killeen.

'For what? As I told you we were sent down here as a team.'

'I mean – you still must be angry with me about what happened out in the White Mountains.'

'No,' Killeen answered. 'I just took you for a green officer in his first campaign, which is what you were.'

'I ordered that village razed,' Calhoun said, remembering back to the day when Killeen had defied his order to burn the Indian camp.

'I recall,' Killeen said. 'I have always held it in mind that if the enemy has to be defeated through the use of arms, then it must be done. But destroying the homes and belongings of civilians can only provoke more hostilities.'

'I see,' Calhoun said, and he seemed to understand Killeen's point finally, yet it still nettled the young officer that his order had been defied by a shaggy, undisciplined civilian. Major Fain had listened later to Calhoun's complaint and unexpectedly taken Killeen's side. That too had irritated Mark Calhoun. He had been taught that the entire concept of battle was to destroy your enemy's ability to wage war. No one had told him that there was a point at which you draw the line between warfare and vengeance.

Killeen had fallen back a little to ride beside the heavily perspiring Thad Folger. The man was obviously now losing all of the nerve he had had.

'It'll go easier on you, Folger, if you come clean with us. We already saw Mingo and some of his band riding toward Westfield.'

'What are you talking about! Who's Mingo?'

'The man wanting to buy the rifles,' Killeen answered, although Folger showed no comprehension. 'If that bunch ever get those Winchesters, dozens of people, soldiers among them will die as a result. If you thought that talk of hanging you was an exaggeration, I can assure you that it wasn't.'

'I don't know anyone called Mingo – I might have heard the name somewhere, I'm not sure,' Folger said, steadily guiding his horse and buggy toward the outskirts of Westfield as the sun rose higher, becoming smaller and hotter in a smoky sky. 'I was dealing with a man named Waco who told me he knew some people with the money to pay for the rifles.'

'Waco?' the name triggered nothing in Killeen's memory although from his days on the border with General Crook a few of the more prominent border raiders were familiar to him. He shook his head. This Waco was apparently a middleman arranging the sale. That, too, was only a guess. Killeen supposed it did not matter. What mattered was finding the rifles and returning them to the army before Mingo obtained them, and they were holding the key to the stolen rifles. Tombstone Jack said he had no memory of where they had hidden them, and Killeen was forced to believe that Jack's addled mind had forgotten what they had done with the weapons.

Folger was another matter. The man, a petty thief obviously ill-equipped for transactions of this size, knew full well where the Winchester '73s were hidden. All they needed just now was a heavy wagon, Folger's continued if reluctant cooperation . . . and a lot of luck.

At Wally Shoup's stable they reined in. The stable owner stood watching them, hands on hips as he instructed a twelve-year-old kid what to do with the wheelbarrow full of manure he had shoveled up from inside the building.

From across the street in front of the Starshine Saloon, Waco's eyes narrowed as he watched Thad Folger draw up his buggy and set the brake. He cursed silently and went inside to find Trevor Steele who was talking with some of the old border gang over beer and whiskey.

'Finished with that horse already?' Shoup asked, stroking the neck of the rented sorrel Lieutenant Calhoun had been riding.

'Haven't even begun,' Mark Calhoun said in a more confident tone than he had used recently.

'We need a wagon,' Killeen said, swinging down from his dun horse.

'There sure has been a run on those lately,' Shoup said, wiping his hands on his jeans. 'You want the same one you had the other night, Mister Folger?' he asked the despondent petty thief. 'The heavier one is the one that Colin Babbit rented the other day to—'

'Either one,' Lieutenant Calhoun said.

Shoup nodded, knowing that no one was going to listen to his tale. He walked around to the back of the stable and began rigging a two-horse team to the wagon Tombstone had used. Shoup wondered if he should invest in another wagon or two. He was getting a lot of calls for rentals these days.

Killeen watched the stable man's flurry of activity for a few minutes, then strolled back to where Lieutenant Calhoun still sat his horse, watching the nervous Thad Folger. 'Now's the time to have a talk with the marshal,' Killeen said. 'Tell him what you think he needs to know.'

'Me?' Mark Calhoun said, apparently surprised.

'Of course, you're practically part of the family. I'll watch our friend here.'

'I have to talk to you, Steele,' Waco said, interrupting a low-stakes poker game his boss was playing with Mingo, Tom Bull and a few of the border riders Waco did not know.

'Is it important, Waco?' Steele asked, giving the thin blond man a glimpse at the hand he was holding: a full house, kings high, sixes under.

'Very,' Waco answered.

'I'll fold, gentlemen,' Trevor Steele said reluctantly, shoving his cards, face-down into the middle of the baize table. Mingo's dark eyes flickered, but he said nothing. He knew Steele well, had played many a card game with him and he knew that the gambler had been holding a good hand.

Steele followed Waco to the front doors of the Starlight, lighting a thin cigar along the way. He said, 'I hope this is important, Waco. You just cost me a few dollars – though I never play for high stakes with friends, especially dangerous friends,' he said, glancing back toward the table where Mingo sat scowling toward the bat-wing doors.

'I think I might have saved you a lot more than you could have won at that table,' Waco said, flushed with pride. 'Look over there at Shoup's stable.'

Steele looked that way, seeing only a man in a buggy talking to a tall, curly-haired stranger. Beyond them an erect young man was crossing the street toward Marshal Slattery's office.

'What are you showing me?' Steele asked with a touch of irritation.

'That's the man! The one in the buggy,' Waco said with urgency. 'He's the one who has the Winchester '73s.'

'You're sure?'

'Of course I'm sure! He's the one who lifted them from the railroad.'

'Who's the man he's talking to?' Steele wanted to know.

'I never saw him before, but something is up, that's for sure.'

And the other man, another stranger, had just entered the marshal's office. Wally Shoup was now leading a heavy wagon around from the back yard of the stable. Something was up for sure. To Steele it smelled of missed opportunity. He couldn't disappoint Mingo now. The border bandit was a terror when disappointed. Steele thought for only a moment.

'Get Tom Bull. I want you two to shadow that wagon wherever it goes.'

EIGHT

Beneath a sultry sky Thad Folger guided the rented wagon out of Westfield once again as Lieutenant Calhoun and Killeen flanked him. Folger had already given up on any idea of trickery. He knew when he had had it, and so he sullenly drove the wagon toward the old Crazy Eights Mine road. Whether the threat of hanging had been only bluff, he did not know, but they could certainly have him locked into the Westfield jail for theft. He was too old to spend weeks, months, years behind bars.

He cursed his fate. But he was not blaming Lieutenant Calhoun or Killeen for his fall, nor himself, but characteristically, the railroad for having fired him in the first place.

An hour on, Folger found the cut-off leading to the old mine and started the team up the steep incline. He himself had worked building this road once, he reflected. Hard work it had been, but it paid well. Before the mine boss had caught him smuggling some high-grade ore off the mountain.

That was the way his luck had always run. The thing with Thad Folger was that he did not understand that any of it could have ever been his own fault. Well, it was all over now one way or the other. He certainly would never be able to work up the nerve to try looting the railroad freights again – he would be watched closely. If he could avoid prosecution for past mistakes. That was the way Folger thought about his crimes – simply *mistakes* he had made.

'There's someone on our trail,' Killeen said to Mark Calhoun as they climbed the rutted road higher into the hills. Calhoun spun in the saddle and peered downward.

'Are you sure?'

'Yes,' Nate Killeen said. 'In this country, in this weather, horses can't help but raise dust in passing.'

'Is it that gang of border raiders we passed?' Calhoun asked, growing nervous.

'It could be a few of them – but I make it out as only two, maybe three horses.'

'What do you think we should do, Killeen.'

'Continue with the mission. But cautiously. It

could be nothing.'

Even Killeen did not believe that. This country was not entirely uninhabited, but it was odd that at this exact time they would find themselves being trailed by a couple of men. Killeen was not a great believer in coincidences.

'Let's do what we came to do,' he told Calhoun. 'I'll drop off at the head of the trail and keep an eye out for trackers.'

'I can't. . . .' Calhoun replied weakly. His confidence seemed to be deflating again.

'If this wart,' Killeen said, nodding toward Folger, 'and an old drunk could lower the rifles, you two should be able to pull them up again.'

'Yes,' Calhoun said, stuttering. Then amazingly, he grinned and added, 'One of these days, I'll learn to start listening to you.'

Reaching the ridge crest where they could see the old tumbledown mine structures, Killeen held them up as he took the Winchester '73 from the back of Thad Folger's wagon.

'Is this loaded?' he asked, then worked the lever to find that indeed it was not. 'What were you going to do with it, wave it at people to frighten them off?'

Folger was in no mood for any sort of conversation. He watched in unhappy silence as Killeen loaded the new rifle with .44-40 rounds from the loops on his gun belt – one of the Winchester's most appealing attributes. Killeen thought that he could have held off a couple of men with his Colt, but having the long gun was definitely desirable.

'I'm going to find a position in those boulders,' Killeen said, indicating the stacked yellow rocks alongside the trail. 'You go about your business. Even if you hear shooting, keep at it. We need to get this done.'

'Where's the hiding place?' Calhoun asked Folger as Killeen, leaving his stoic dun to graze on a patch of yellowed buffalo grass, began climbing the boulders.

'Right over there,' Folger said, growing more morose by the hour. 'I'll show you.'

'You'd better,' Mark Calhoun said quietly, but finely. 'You've got a lot riding on this, you know.'

'I know,' Folger grumbled with a touch of irritation. Familiarly, he guided the team across the dead mining camp to the long disused shaft where he and Tombstone Jack had hidden the shipment of army rifles.

'Right here,' Folger said, halting the team.

'Where? I don't see anything,' Calhoun answered.

'That hole up there,' Folger said with weariness. 'We put those rocks over the lines we lowered the crates with.'

'Very clever,' Calhoun said.

'It seemed so at the time,' Folger replied.

'Well, climb down and let's get to work,' Mark Calhoun said. His eyes flickered toward the rocks where Killeen had disappeared, wondering if they were about to be stormed by a gang of border raiders.

They bent to their task, kicking away the covering rocks or clawing at them until they found the concealed ropes. The sun grew hotter on their backs; the air seemed drier in their lungs. Folger obviously was not used to this kind of work. Mark Calhoun, twenty years younger, struggled. To the west, at the head of the trail, a single searching shot was fired. Killeen had found his targets.

'Get a move on,' Calhoun urged Folger who seemed about to faint from the exertion and the heat. They now had the ropes uncovered – there were six of them in all, two lines for each of the shipping crates. Calhoun collected the first pair and handed one of the lines to Folger who stood perspiring, ashen. From across the old mining camp they heard two more rapidly fired shots.

They bent to their task, drawing on the lines. Mark Calhoun wondered how deep the shaft was as he labored at pulling the heavy weight of the crate up. Folger stood beside him, panting. Suddenly Mark felt the palms of his hand burning, losing skin as the crate fell away, slipping with blistering speed through his hands. Folger had let go of his line. The man looked suddenly unwell. From the boulders Mark heard three more reports from Killeen's rifle and two answering shots from below.

'Damnit!' Calhoun snarled, 'we have to get this done – for everyone's sake!'

'I just don't know if I can,' Folger protested, looking at his own hands. 'I'm not a young man anymore.'

Calhoun started to issue a sharp retort, thought better of it and tried to put himself in a more experienced officer's boots. What to do? Of course!

'I'm going to back the wagon in. Then we'll tie all six lines on to the axle. Got it?' As another shot was fired from the rocky knoll, Folger only nodded dismally. Calhoun mounted the wagon box and backed the well-trained horses to within range of the ropes, set the brake and leaped down to help the fumbling Thad Folger knot the lines around the rear axle of the rented wagon. What if the horses could not draw the weight out of the depths of the mine shaft? Worse, what if the strain caused the axle to break? There was nothing to do but try it and hope for the best. Hadn't Folger ever given any thought as to how he was going to recover the hidden weapons?

The plan worked. It was simply done. The team without strain pulled up the three crates from the depths of the shaft. One crate was split open, but not destroyed. The other two looked as good as they did on the day they were assembled, though a little scuffed and dirty.

From the head of the trail more shots could be heard.

'Let's get these loaded up quickly,' Lieutenant Calhoun said.

'How are we supposed to get out of here?' Folger asked.

'Is there another trail down?'

'Not suitable for a wagon and team,' Folger said, not fearfully, but with weariness. Thad Folger had had enough of his own schemes, it seemed.

'We'll have to talk to Killeen and find out what the situation is,' Calhoun said.

Even as Calhoun spoke, Killeen, seeing that they had retrieved the crates, was clambering down from among the boulders. At Calhoun's approach he stood in the center of the road, holding the reins to his horse.

'I'm pretty sure that I plugged one of them,' Killeen said. 'The second rider gave it up. He's either hiding down there or he's scattered for home.'

'You think we can risk the trail?' Mark asked.

'I don't think there's any other choice,' Killeen told him. 'We're in a trap if we stay here and other riders come along.'

'You're right, of course,' Calhoun agreed. 'How do we handle it?'

'I'll take the lead,' Killeen said. 'Let Folger drive the wagon – he knows there's nowhere to run now. You bring up the rear.'

'All right, general,' Lieutenant Calhoun replied. Killeen couldn't detect any mockery in his voice. If it was intended, it made no difference. They had to get down out of the hills, and fast. Killeen had no idea where Mingo and his men were, but if the raiders knew that the rifles had been recovered, they would be on their way in a matter of minutes.

Waco lay concealed in a clump of tightly-woven chaparral – sumac, sage and manzanita – alongside the wagon road. His shoulder had at first throbbed with fiery pain, now it only throbbed and itched – itched terribly. He knew he had been lucky. The marksman in the rocks had only nicked him. The mysterious Tom Bull had taken one full in the chest.

Tom had always been a trustworthy ally in a fight.

They called him 'Mysterious Tom' because he had never given even his closest companions the story of his life. It was said that he had been a Union soldier during the War, had seen the depredations of William Tecumseh Sherman on his march to the sea, the looting and sacking, become sickened by it and tried to transfer his allegiance to the Rebel cause. Captured as a spy, he had been sent to Andersonville prison where after months of suffering he had escaped with a handful of other prisoners and made his way West, leaving the war temporarily behind.

But it had caught up with Tom Bull again, and he had joined up with Quantrill's Kansas raiders until he saw the savagery of those men, which was reminiscent of Sherman's army. He decided that he had no loyalties left, and so Tom Bull had aligned himself with the renegade border raiders under Trevor Steele.

Tom Bull was plain and simple – a fighting man looking for a just war and unable to find one.

Now the mysterious man was dead, never having given up his secrets. The sniper above them in the rocks had directed a rifle bullet into Tom's heart. Waco did not feel anger, but the icy fingers of fear were beginning to scratch at his spine as he lay in the hot dust alongside the road, hearing the wagon approach.

Waco had not ever thought of himself as a coward, but wasn't there always a time when a man has to admit he has had enough? Big old Tom Bull, his eyes wide-open had just flopped back to lie staring at the empty sky. Waco had decided at that moment that he did not want to go out that way, not for a few rifles, not for Mingo or for Trevor Steele. He buried his face against his forearms and waited while the horses above him clopped past along the trail.

'Where are they then?' Mingo asked finally after the last hand had been played. He had accepted one of Trevor Steele's thin cigars and now was lighting it. 'The game was fine, the whiskey is good, but this is not what I came here for, *hombre*.'

'I sent Waco and Tom Bull out to bring them in,' Steele lied easily.

'And if the local law should become curious about my presence?' Mingo asked.

'No one knows who you are. Besides the marshal is a fat fool.'

'People have been killed by fat fools,' Mingo said significantly. 'I don't mean to be. Show me the rifles; tell me your price; let me ride away.'

'You don't trust me, old friend!' Steele said with a wide smile.

'Once a man has left the gang, you can no longer afford trust,' Mingo said, his dark eyebrows drawing together. 'I think you have gone soft,' he added. 'The way you dress – the way you live. You have made me promises. You must be expected to keep them, Steele.'

'Of course,' Trevor Steele answered. 'It is all taken care of. I promise you.' Steele smiled again, but if a man can sweat internally, that was exactly what Steele was doing at that moment. He could read the threat in Mingo's eyes, and he had no idea how Tom Bull and Waco had made out on their assignment. 'Just be patient for a little longer – would you like to have a meal or take a turn at the roulette wheel?'

Mingo did not answer, nor did his scowling expression change. He summoned Herb Blake to the table with only a gesture of his eyes. He whispered something into Blake's ear and the badly scarred little man nodded.

Steele, like Thad Folger, was beginning to wish he had not gotten himself mixed up in this business.

'We need to take the train,' Nate Killeen said as they neared the outskirts of Westfield.

'What?'

'We need to transfer the rifles to the train. We

won't have much chance if we try taking the wagon across country and Mingo figures out where we've gone. We'll go around to the back of the depot, then I'll find out when the next freight is coming through.'

'All right,' Lieutenant Calhoun said wearily. He was again ready to surrender his mantle of command to Killeen. Folger, who knew the way well, followed the river road to the depot and pulled up in the shade of the storage shed. Killeen swung down from his dun horse.

'I'll talk to Garrett, or if he's not here, to Toby, the ticket agent. They'll be able to tell us when the next westbound train is due. Watch Folger and the rifles and yell out if you see trouble coming.' Killeen added, as if in all seriousness; 'And, Lieutenant, no women for now.'

Mark Calhoun wasn't sure how to take the remark. He only nodded and swung down himself in the heated shade as Killeen made his way to the front of the depot, crossing the platform. He almost walked into Tombstone Jack.

'Hello, Jack,' Killeen said with surprise. 'I had the idea you'd be out of action for awhile.'

'Wish I was,' Jack said unhappily, 'but Garrett told me I'm still hired on; I thought I'd better work my regular shift.'

'Is Garrett here now?'

'He's inside?' Jack asked with narrowing eyes. 'What's going on?'

'Nothing much. I just to need to arrange for a small shipment to Fort Thomas.'

'You don't mean you got them back!' Jack asked in astonishment. Killeen only winked an eye in response. As Killeen went on his way toward the station master's office Tombstone sought out one of his familiar hidey-holes, reaching for the flask on his hip.

'Not until three o'clock!' Quentin Garrett was saying. Killeen nodded.

'That'll have to do then. Passage for two men and their horses and three crates of army material.'

'It's not,' Garrett said uneasily, wiping his forehead with his white handkerchief, 'anything that is going to cause an uproar, I hope – this shipment?'

'Mr Garrett,' Killeen answered, 'I certainly hope not.'

'Well?' Mingo demanded. The scrawny, scarred Herb Blake stood before the leader of the border raiders in his small hotel room, trail dusty and perspiring.

'They brought the rifles back to town,' Blake answered.

'Who?' Mingo was in a foul mood. 'Steele's men

– Waco and Tom Bull?'

'No. Three men I've never seen before. They took them directly to the railroad depot.'

'Are you sure?'

'I followed them all the way, Mingo.'

'Then we've got to take them at the depot. We can't ride down a freight train and stop it on the desert once it gets up to speed.'

'No,' Blake agreed. 'What do you want me to do, Mingo?'

'Gather the boys, tell them to stop whatever they're doing – drinking, gambling, womanizing – and be ready for some work. Three men, did you say, Blake?'

'That was all – three men. Unless they were meeting others at the railroad station.'

'That's all right, then,' Mingo said. The bandit leader was at the window now, thumbs hooked into his gunbelt as he stared out at the streets of Westfield. 'I wish we had the whole gang with us, but we're enough of a force. We've got to get there before the train pulls out, though. You'd better scoot and round the boys up.'

'What about Steele? He might have a few men he can loan us,' Herb Blake suggested.

'Steele is out of this now,' Mingo said, turning to face Blake with a ferocious expression. 'He had his chance to come through and he let me down. Now we do it on our own; I'll talk to Steele later. On my own. Get out of here now, Blake – do as I told you. I want those rifles,' Mingo said threateningly. 'That's what I came here for. I will have them.'

NINE

On a whim Marshal Slattery decided to amble past the railroad station on this heated morning. He seldom paid the place a visit, but there seemed to be a lot of activity over there these days. Mark Calhoun, of whom he found himself growing fonder, had come to his office earlier and they had had a visit during which Calhoun had outlined the situation. Stolen rifles. The army trying to recover them. The young officer seemed to have some nerve, and Slattery could even forgive the man for courting his daughter. Slattery had thought of the life a young woman must endure in bandit country, but Marie could do a lot worse, Slattery supposed upon reflection. A loyal and brave officer. Mark Calhoun was handsome enough, and well set-up so that Slattery could see how Marie could be smitten with him.

It could be worse, Slattery told himself now. Suppose she had fallen for one of these local idlers, drifters or a gambler . . . and thinking along these lines, he happened to encounter Trevor Steele as he strode the plankwalk.

Steele – now there was a man Marshal Slattery never trusted. He had shifty eyes that held a glint as if he believed he were smarter than anyone else in the world. A foxy man with a shadowy background. Steele touched the brim of his white hat with two fingers and walked on, deep in thought, it seemed.

The marshal continued toward the depot, having come slowly to a decision – if Marie wanted to marry the young officer he would withdraw his objections. Perhaps it was a perilous sort of life, but the army had pensions for widows, did it not?

Steele had met up with Waco when the thin young blond man managed to drag himself into town after the shoot-out at the Crazy Eights Mine. Minutes before, Mingo had told him that Steele was out of any deal they had cut. Mingo would take care of matters himself. That was a lot of money gone missing. Too much to lose out on. Waco had been advised to have himself treated for his wound and then to round up as many of the men who had remained loyal to Steele as he could find. There was shooting trouble coming.

That done, Trevor Steele had briefly walked past the depot and seen the wagon with three suspicious-looking crates in its bed. Thad Folger, the man identified as the initiator of the robbery, sat on the buckboard, his face folded between his hands dismally. That settled it in Steele's mind. The other two men, whoever they were, were army agents, and the freight was going out on the next train. He made his way steadily toward Wally Shoup's stable.

Flashing his brilliant smile, Steele entered the dark barn and told Shoup, 'I need to rent a team and wagon.'

Wally Shoup mentally reminded himself that his business was picking up so quickly these days that maybe it would be worthwhile to invest in a couple more wagons and dray horses.

As Wally hitched the team, Trevor Steele stood smoking his cigar, silently brooding. If Mingo thought that Steele had lost his touch, and that was the reason he had handed over the reins of the border raiders to Mingo, the man had a lot to learn. Steele still had a few tricks up his sleeve as Mingo was about to find out.

At 11:45 that morning, fifteen minutes before the bank examiners were due to arrive, Henry Crimson made his way back into the vault of his bank. Colin Babbit had never returned; he must be dead. The deal for the army rifles had fallen through. Crimson looped a rope around the steel cross-beam of the vault and tightened the knotted end around his neck. Standing on a wooden chair he closed his eyes and jumped from it. He made a series of strange gurgling sounds, but no one was there to see or hear his last protest against his own existence.

Marshal Slattery was nearly to the railroad depot when he noticed the knot of men in the alley beside the Starshine Saloon. He didn't know who they were, but Lieutenant Calhoun had warned him that there might be a gang of border raiders in Westfield. There was no way of telling if these were the men, but a band of unwashed strangers grouped together like that, all well-armed, was enough to cause Slattery to begin worrying. He hurried on toward the depot.

Coming up on the warehouse side of the structure, he saw Thad Folger sitting on a wagon seat, horses still and ears twitching as flies annoyed them. Folger had his head in his hands. Slattery knew of the rumors about Thad Folger of course – he was a little more alert than people around Westfield seemed to give him credit for. However, he had always looked upon Folger's petty theft as railroad business.

Behind the wagon stood Mark Calhoun wearing an unhappy expression. Mark glanced up as he saw Slattery approaching heavily, his great belly rolling from side to side.

'Hello, Harold,' Mark said, now feeling comfortable enough in his relationship with Marie and her father to use the marshal's first name.

'I think you might have some trouble on the way,' Slattery said in a panting voice. He whipped off his hat and wiped at his brow as Calhoun waited. Folger had heard Slattery's words and his head came up and turned toward them with an unhappy expression. Mark waited until Slattery was able to go on.

'I passed a gang of men – I don't know who they were – I think they might be headed this way,' the marshal said.

'Can you describe them?'

'Big men, little men, a couple of Mexicans, I think,' was all Slattery could say unhelpfully.

'We have got to get these rifles on to the three o'clock train,' Calhoun said as if pained. 'It is imperative. I wonder if they know the train schedule.'

'You can wonder a lot of things,' Slattery said, 'but that won't provide us with any answers. Best thing to do is find a defensible position and be ready.'

'I suppose so,' Mark Calhoun said. 'Do me a favor and keep an eye out, will you, Harold? I've got to find Killeen and tell him what's happening.'

Scurrying off, up on to the platform and around the corner, Calhoun found Killeen still in the station master's office. Calhoun burst in, paused, glancing at the clock on the wall, and told Killeen, 'The marshal thinks we have trouble. The border raiders may know where the rifles are, and plan on capturing them.'

Killeen muttered an indistinct curse. Quentin Garrett said loudly, 'I won't have gunplay at my station – you'll have to get away from here!'

'We can't do that,' Lieutenant Calhoun said. 'Army orders. We have to load those rifles. Is there any way to advise the railroad crew that we may have trouble brewing?'

'Not if they've already left the Tamarind Springs stop.' He glanced at the clock on the wall himself, and added dismally, 'And they have.'

'Don't you have some sort of emergency signal?' Killeen asked.

'I could red-flag them,' the station master told them, 'but that's the signal to keep on rolling through no matter what. It wouldn't help you with your problem.'

'No,' Killeen agreed. 'None at all.' He asked Mark Calhoun, 'Did the marshal tell you how many men we might be up against?'

'No, he didn't. I suppose it must be that band of men we passed earlier.'

'Five or six. It all depends on how badly Mingo wants those rifles.' Killeen paused, and strangely, smiled. 'Well, we do have the advantage on them. . . .'

'We do?'

'Sure! We're all going to be armed with new Winchester '73s,' the scout said with a thin smile. 'Is there anyone around who can help us out, Garrett?'

'No, there's only me and Toby . . . and Tombstone is around somewhere.'

'All right,' Killeen said, satisfied. 'I'll take Tombstone. That gives us five men armed with Winchester repeaters. You and Toby can sit this one out.'

Garrett's face brightened with relief. 'I'll find Tombstone!' he said eagerly.

'And now?' Calhoun asked Killeen.

'And now, let's pry open one of those crates and clean those rifles up. If Mingo is really on his way, we'll need all the firepower we can get.'

*

Trevor Steele watched sullenly as Mingo led his band of rough men along the main street of Westfield and turned into an alley leading toward the Arizona & Eastern depot. Steele was briefly unsure of his own plan to recover the rifles, but about then Waco arrived with six men who had remained loyal to Steele after Mingo had assumed command of the border gang.

'What's going on?' Waco wanted to know. 'I saw Mingo marching toward the depot.'

'He's going to try to take them right now, in the middle of town. I don't think he'll get away with it. The man never has showed restraint when it was needed. For the moment, we can only watch and wait. Get all of the men mounted and ready to ride. We're headed toward Comanche Wells.'

'If Mingo wins. . . ?' Waco asked.

'Then we change plans. I will track him down. The man cut me out of the deal – if he succeeds, I'm cutting *him* out.'

'Trevor,' Waco said nervously. 'If we do this, we'll pretty much have no choice but to go back to riding with the gang again.'

'Then,' Steele said philosophically, 'all I can say is that we've had a good vacation.'

Killeen had set his people up as well as he could. The reluctant Folger – induced by a promise of leniency – and a surprisingly eager Tombstone Jack, both equipped with the new Winchester '73, were positioned to the right and left, Jack in the window of the depot, Folger in the storage shed. Killeen had unharnessed the horse team after turning the wagon broadside to the alley, and behind it he, Calhoun and Marshal Slattery, who had volunteered saying, 'This is my town!' had taken up their positions.

Killeen felt that they had every advantage over Mingo, all of them with shelter and armed with repeating rifles, but as he knew too well, something could always go wrong in a firefight. They waited in the heated afternoon beneath a sky seemingly sheeted over with a white veil. Inside the depot, Garrett had been delegated to keep all onlookers away or take them into shelter. The arrival of any train in the West was still an event that drew observers.

'How much time?' Calhoun asked as Killeen, perspiring through his red shirt, crouched beside him, thumbing fresh loads into his Winchester.

'It was quarter to two the last time I saw a clock,' Killeen answered.

'Quarter after now,' Harold Slattery said, holding up his steel pocket watch.

'How much time. . . ?' Calhoun said again, his

voice low but controlled. Killeen guessed that the young officer's question was not about the time of day, but how much time he had before Mingo and his men arrived, how much longer he might have to live, or perhaps about how long he had before he could return to his beloved Marie.

Those were questions that Killeen could not answer.

'Some men coming!' Tombstone Jack called out from his post at the window of the depot building.

'Is it them?' Marshal Slattery wanted to know.

'Sure looks like it!'

Raising his eyes above the wagon bed, Killeen saw three, five men tramping around the corner of the alley entrance in a group. That was good – it meant that Mingo had not given any thought to flanking them. For it was Mingo. With his ruffled white shirt and huge black mustache he was identifiable even at that distance.

'Let them get closer,' Killeen said to Calhoun who held his rifle nervously, aimed at the alley head. 'We've got the time and the numbers.'

'How much time?' Calhoun asked, and Killeen glanced at the young officer, hoping his nerve would hold out.

Killeen thought briefly about calling out a warning, realized that it would defeat their purpose to do so. He also reminded himself of the type of men he was facing – killers, thieves, predators. Mingo and his men marched toward them, unaware of the ambush. Finally, Killeen said quietly but audibly, 'Let them have it, boys.'

Oddly, no sooner had the words left his throat than the Mingo Gang opened up first. One of the men – it was Herb Blake – had spotted the glint of sunlight on a rifle barrel in the storage shed where Thad Folger was stationed. Blake drew his Colt and fired three rounds at the window, sending Folger diving toward the floor.

Tombstone Jack was not so shy. From his position in the depot window he levered through half a dozen shots which sent the band of raiders scattering. One bullet tagged Blake and he dropped, sprawled against the white dust of the alley. To his right, as he shouldered his rifle, Killeen could see the horse team rearing up with panic and he was doubly glad that he had unhitched them. Beside him, Calhoun opened up with a barrage of fire. Out of a sense of urgency or of self-preservation. He must have put ten shots through the barrel of the Winchester before pausing.

Killeen saw two more Mingo men drop. Mingo himself dove behind an empty water barrel, firing wildly in their direction with his pistol. Marshal

Slattery, eyes narrowed, took his time in aiming. He got Mingo with his second shot. The mustached man flapped his hands wildly in the air before crumbling to the ground. His own prophecy had been fulfilled: fat men can certainly kill you as well as anyone.

Folger, either infuriated or simply regaining his courage, was firing as well, and Killeen saw a fourth border raider go down. The fifth seemed to have fled the battlefield. Killeen himself had not pulled the trigger on his own weapon. It did not matter to him – it had not been a contest. Now he rose from his position and cautiously strode the alleyway, searching for survivors. There were none. He toed the still figures of Blake and Mingo and then waved his hat in the air as a signal and one by one his men emerged from concealment.

Only Tombstone Jack had been nicked, and it was a very slight crease across his shoulder.

'We'll get you to a doctor,' Killeen offered.

'I prefer to treat myself,' Jack said. He handed his borrowed Winchester over to Killeen and reached for his flask as he limped away.

In the distance a train whistle sounded.

Trevor Steele stood near the stable, listening to the gunfire at the depot. His ears told him what was happening. The sharp report of four or five Winchesters answered the duller echoes of six-guns. After a minute, a man known to Steele only as Purdy, burst from the alleyway and raced on down the street to where his horse was hitched at the Starshine Saloon.

'They got Mingo,' Steele said to Waco who was trying to put on a new shirt over his bandaged shoulder. 'We're all right, then. Can you ride?'

'I don't know,' the blond gunman said uneasily as he buttoned his shirt.

'Handle the wagon?' Steele asked.

'Sure.'

'All right, then. Get going. We'll meet you at Comanche Wells. I'm going to show the ghost of Mingo how these things should be handled.'

TEN

When the train pulled in right on the dot at 3 p.m., Killeen and Lieutenant Calhoun were there waiting to meet it. They had let Folger go his own way, as promised. Tombstone Jack and his flask were nowhere to be seen. Marshal Slattery had ambled off to arrange the business of cleaning up the carnage around the depot after having a private conversation with Mark Calhoun, assuring the young officer that he would be welcomed into the family.

'I'm glad that's over with,' Calhoun admitted to Killeen as they waited for the engineer to shut down the train.

'It's not over until the money's in the bank,' Killeen said.

'I don't get you,' Calhoun said irritably. 'The raiders are all dead. Nothing can go wrong now!'

'Old son,' Killeen answered, 'something can always go wrong.'

The engineer – Frank Ames again – Joe Cox and a man Killeen hadn't seen before were climbing down from the cab of the locomotive, planning on their usual dinner at the Blue Bird Café.

Approaching, Killeen told them, 'Sorry, no lunch today, boys.'

'It's on our schedule,' Ames objected.

'This is what you might call an army emergency – that is, we've got those stolen rifles and they have to get to Fort Thomas as soon as possible.'

'Can't they wait?' Joe Cox, the little stump of a fireman asked.

'They've already waited,' Killeen replied. 'Help us get them aboard this freight. We have to leave as soon as possible.'

Frank Ames who was used to having his schedule interrupted for any number of reasons, agreed, but reminded Killeen, 'We'll still have to stop at Comanche Wells for water.'

'There's no one minding the station, is there?'

'No, but they still have water. We can fill the boiler ourselves, it wouldn't be the first time. In the old days. . . .' He continued on, but Killeen was not interested in old times at that moment; he just wanted to get those rifles delivered to Major Fain at Fort Thomas before taking a week's furlough. A week's sleep.

They unlocked one of the freight cars and lugged the three crates aboard – one of them had been opened, of course, broken first by Folger taking a rifle for his own use, then in the retrieval from the mine shaft and later for Killeen and his men to arm themselves against Mingo, but the major would understand that when it was explained.

That was only a small matter. Killeen and Calhoun both breathed a sigh of relief when the weapons were finally on board, their horses led up a ramp and loaded into the last freight car. The battle was very nearly won.

Walking back toward the locomotive, Killeen was bantering with the engineer, Ames. 'How do you handle this job? Going back and forth and never really getting anywhere?'

'Like everyone else, you mean?' Frank Ames answered with a rare smile. 'I don't know, Killeen, I suppose the job's a little repetitive, but I get a paycheck along the way. Besides,' he added, placing a hand on the solid steel of the beast he drove, 'I love this old iron horse. We're changing the face of the nation one trip at a time. Let's get going! I don't much care for the grub at Fort Thomas, but my stomach doesn't care if it's fancy or not so long as it's filled.'

'Where do we ride?' Calhoun wanted to know.

'I can carry one more man in the cab,' Ames said. 'Maybe one of you should ride in the car with the rifles.'

'I'll do that,' Killeen volunteered, though not happily, and so as Calhoun climbed up into the locomotive cab he made his way back to the freight car, got aboard and settled uneasily on one of the rifle crates, closing the door behind him, but leaving a little room for air and a view of the country beyond.

The train started with a jerk and the clanging of its brass bell. Killeen was nearly thrown to the floor and he braced himself as the train continued forward with a series of fits and starts before gathering speed and beginning its smooth, powerful glide along the steel rails.

Comanche Wells – their first and only stop along the way before they reached Fort Thomas – Killeen had a bad feeling about the station. Perhaps that was only because of his memory of what had happened there previously, but he would be glad to fill the boiler and be gone from the place.

Mingo was dead, his band killed or dispersed, but one never knew, as he had told Mark Calhoun, *It's not over until the money is in the bank.* Who was to say that Mingo, who reputedly had thirty or more men riding with him had not planned on the contingency of his raid at Westfield failing and sent more bandits on ahead to Comanche Wells.

Killeen doubted that scenario. He and Calhoun had passed Mingo as he entered Westfield, and his band of men was small, the same number they had encountered in the depot shoot-out – and the raid at Comanche Wells had apparently occurred before Mingo's arrival. Who then? Killeen scolded himself for not having spent more time interrogating Thad Folger who knew more about this business than anyone else but there had never been the time.

It was all probably a false concern. With any luck this day would involve nothing more than stopping at Comanche Wells for water, reaching Fort Thomas, reporting to Major Fain, and going to sleep for a long, long time.

Trevor Steele and his half-dozen men were on schedule to reach Comanche Wells before the train. Again using the Pine Bluff cut-off, they could occasionally glimpse the train through the screen of lodgepole pines, making its way across the flat desert.

Waco did not look good, and Steele was concerned. Maybe he should have left the blond man behind. He seemed to have gotten blood poisoning from the lead he had taken at the Crazy Eights Mine shoot-out. Waco rode pale and limp in the saddle, continuing it seemed out of obligation. The other men were boisterous, eager to ride. Some of them were still half-drunk. They weren't the companions Steele would have chosen in earlier times, but these were the best he could come up with on short notice.

He reflected as he rode – as Waco had commented – after this payday, which promised to be a big one, they would have little choice but to rejoin the border raiders. It wasn't the future Steele had planned for himself, but then nothing ever went precisely as planned. It might not be too bad. When word of Mingo's death reached the raiders, they might welcome their old general back with open arms. With the proceeds from the sale of the stolen rifles to the highest bidder, Steele could bide his time, organize a few low-risk raids and after a time, slip away again.

He had fallen too much in love with his soft life as a gambler. Let a younger man take control of the gang. Hell, he thought with a smile, they have gambling in Mexico as well.

For the time being, he had to concentrate on the day's work ahead of him. The last time they had gone in ill-prepared for their assault on the train, expecting no resistance. Of course that time they hadn't known that the rifles were not on board as promised. This time they *did* know for sure that the Winchesters were aboard. But this time, too, Steele did expect some resistance. The two strangers – Steele took them for out-of-uniform soldiers, detailed to recover the weapons. There were those two and the train crew who had unexpectedly put up a short battle with them the last time.

Who else? There would be no station crew at Comanche Wells, he thought. The railroad could hardly have had time to replace the two men shot down there. An army patrol? No – why would one be sent from Fort Thomas when they expected the shipment to arrive within hours aboard the fast freight?

Still, one never knew. The station at Comanche Wells was already in sight, and Steele broke off his thoughts. All he could do now was position his men and wait for the train, still distantly visible on the desert flats. This raid would require some caution, but it could be accomplished. It would be – Trevor

Steele had no intention of going out as Mingo had.

Nate Killeen had grown tired of staring out at the monotonous flat scenery; indeed he had almost fallen asleep when Frank Ames began throttling down, touching the brake as the freight train approached the seemingly deserted Comanche Wells station. The high sun had begun its slow descent toward the western mountains and shadows were long and deep beside the train as it slowed and prepared to stop beside the water tank. Killeen caught a glimpse of the station building, its few surrounding willow trees, and. . . .

A glimpse of a rapidly scurrying man, diving for shelter behind an outbuilding. The raiders were there, then Lieutenant Calhoun, stepping from the confines of the locomotive cab, stretched as the trainmen began to lower the huge filler pipe from the water tower. He walked back to where Killeen was hidden and slid the freight car door open.

'Get in. Quick!' Killeen said. 'They're out there.'

'Who?' Calhoun asked, scrambling aboard quickly, knocking a knee in the process.

'I don't know,' Killeen said, 'but I saw someone.'

'Shouldn't I tell the train crew?'

'Are they armed?'

'No.'

'I thought not – besides our prime directive is to protect these rifles. Unless they're mad, the bandits won't gun down an unarmed train crew.'

'I suppose not,' Calhoun said. There was disappointment on his face. He had believed the battle had ended back in Westfield. 'What do we do, Killeen?'

'Fort up – we couldn't ask for a better place to hold them off.'

No, the sides of the freight car were probably impervious to gunfire, though the idea of being under siege did not appeal to Calhoun.

'If anyone moves, we've got them in our sights. We aren't likely to be picked off in here,' Killeen said as if continuing an internal dialogue with himself. 'Drag those crates over here; we'll set up a little parapet for ourselves.'

'And then?'

'And then we settle in for a long battle.' Killeen smiled again. 'They might have the numbers, but we've got the weaponry. A lot of it.'

The crates were hastily drawn into position, and no sooner had they been stacked than Killeen saw the same bandit peering out from behind the outbuilding. Killeen shouldered his borrowed Winchester and put a slug into the wooden wall of the building beside the man's ear, spraying his face with splinters.

It had begun.

'Maybe you shouldn't have done that, Killeen – let them know where we are.'

'Maybe I should have just let him sneak up on the train,' Killeen said, working the smooth lever action of the Winchester.

'No . . . I'm sorry.'

'No need for an apology. Just stay alert, Calhoun. We don't know who they are or how many of them are out there, but we know they'll be coming.'

'The train will be rolling soon,' Calhoun said hopefully.

'I doubt it. If this is as well-planned as I think, they'll already have rounded up the crew.' Killeen frowned. 'No, we're stuck on the tracks. They may wait until dark, but you can bet they'll be coming.'

'When the train is late getting into Fort Thomas, they'll—'

'They'll what?' Killeen asked more sharply than intended. 'Every day there's a hundred things that can happen to delay a train.'

'I know that,' Calhoun said as if angry with himself.

'Grab a rifle, then. I don't think this bunch is going to give it up.'

*

At the front of the train Frank Ames and his two-man crew had been surrounded by Steele's raiders. Hands hoisted high, they were forced to the old depot building and shoved inside. Trevor Steele smiled with satisfaction. That left his six men against the two army personnel. The odds were in his favor. The trick, obviously, was how to get at them inside the freight car.

He thought he knew.

'Gather up some wood, boys,' he said, 'we're going to have to burn them out.'

The outlaws, lazy if it came to anything other than squeezing the triggers of their guns, grumbled but complied. One man, more careless than the rest, walked to the north side of the train, scouring the ground. He walked directly into Killeen's sight, and Killeen showing no mercy on men obviously intent on killing him and Calhoun, triggered off a well-aimed shot which caught the man in mid-stride and sent him face first into the ground.

'That's one,' Calhoun said.

'There won't be any others making that mistake,' Nate Killeen said.

'What are they up to?'

'That one was gathering wood. I suspect they're

going to try to build a fire under us.'

'Good God!' Calhoun breathed. 'They'll destroy the rifles too.'

'Flesh burns a lot quicker than steel,' Killeen said. 'And those rifles don't need to breathe.'

'It's inhuman!' Calhoun protested.

'What led you to believe that the border raiders were human?'

'What can we do?' the young lieutenant asked.

'Don't know yet. I've one idea – we know they're going to try to set the blaze on the opposite side of the train. So who does that leave on this side?'

'Are you saying we go out and face them?'

'We're going to have to get out of here sooner or later,' Killeen replied. 'I think we should try it now, before we're burned out.'

'I don't like it,' Mark Calhoun said.

'I don't like it either, but I can't see that we have an option.'

No, just leaping out into open ground with guns all around them did not seem like a good plan, but it beat being incinerated.

'When?' Calhoun asked almost breathlessly.

'Right now – we know they're scouring the area for fuel. If we sprint for the side of the depot we should be able to make it across to that outbuilding. Remember, Lieutenant, we still do have an advantage. Fill the tube of that Winchester. If we reach the outbuilding, we should be able to do some real damage.'

'If we don't reach it—?' Calhoun said shakily.

'For myself, almost anything beats being burned to death,' Killeen answered. 'Let's give it a try.'

'You have a lot of courage, Killeen,' Calhoun said with genuine respect.

The scout laughed unexpectedly. 'I have a lot of fear,' he countered. 'Let's get to it.'

Sliding the freight car door open on its iron tracks they received no incoming shots. They leaped from the train, Killeen first, and raced toward the side of the depot building. Someone shouted from near the locomotive and a single shot was winged their way. Ducking reflexively, Killeen sprinted toward the outbuilding – a tenuously constructed storage shed, and reached the corner of it before a series of shots slammed into its wooden walls. Panting, he drew up, watching as Calhoun dove behind its shelter as well.

'Now what?' Calhoun asked from one knee.

'Now, old son, we give 'em hell.'

Positioning himself, Winchester at his shoulder, he levered through three rapid shots. The first man who rounded the nose of the locomotive in their direction took a hit in the neck and staggered back, clutching at this throat, his Springfield rifle falling free to clatter on the rails. The numbers were getting better, more to Killeen's liking.

The opposing fire stilled as the outlaws paused – probably to formulate a plan of attack.

Killeen said urgently, 'Take the other corner of the building! They're up to something.'

Calhoun had barely reached the opposite corner when he spotted a bandit dashing through the dry willow trees in their direction. The man was slender, blond, seemingly already injured. It was no time to show mercy. Calhoun drew a bead with his Winchester and shot Waco dead.

How many left? Calhoun counted three of the raiders already out of action. Three against two – still not good, but they had the superior weapons. As he ran mentally through his calculations, he heard Killeen trigger off four rapid rounds from his repeating rifle. He believed the odds had just gotten better.

Killeen did not miss his shots.

In truth Killeen had taken one man down and wounded another as they charged recklessly at his position. Men without names, dying futilely – just like any other battle in mankind's history.

Trevor Steele watched his men go down and made his decision – to hell with the rifles! There were other ways to make money. He had underestimated his enemy and overestimated his little army. A tactical withdrawal was called for. He circled the depot and dashed into the willows where he had left his horse tethered. He wanted out of there.

ELEVEN

'There he goes!' Killeen shouted as Trevor Steele spurred his horse away from the depot.

'Who is it?'

'I don't know. Their leader, I suppose. The generals are always the first to withdraw. Get to the railroad crew and have them start moving that train toward Fort Thomas.'

'What are you going to do?' Calhoun asked.

'What do you think? I'm going after him.'

Lieutenant Calhoun watched in astonishment. The raider, whoever he was, had a good lead on Killeen and before Killeen could find a ramp and unload his horse, it would be lengthened dramatically. Calhoun trotted toward the depot to tell the railroad crew that it was safe to come out. Calhoun had taken six long strides before he saw Killeen, not bothering with a ramp, leap his little dun pony from the railroad car to follow after the robber. Neither of them had bothered to unsaddle their horses for the short trip to Fort Thomas – that had saved Killeen another few minutes, and now as he rode out, bent low over the withers of the dun horse, he was practically in the trailing dust of the escaping outlaw. Shaking his head in admiration, Calhoun continued on his mission.

Killeen didn't hesitate. The man riding ahead of him had shown no inclination to halt and exchange gunfire. He was stretching out his horse at a dead run, and a quick horse it was. But Killeen wasn't worried. He knew his own horse. The balky little dun was not swift or handsome, but it could run all day, and it was relatively well-rested now.

Ahead Killeen could see a land form he recognized as the low plateau they called Pine Bluff. The bandit leader was heading directly toward it, perhaps wanting the high ground to defend himself. Only once did the fleeing man glance back across his shoulder as if measuring his lead. It was still considerable, but his roan horse now seemed to be faltering. Killeen thought that once they started climbing the bluff, his dun could make up more ground, despite the roan's longer legs.

The roan was definitely tiring as the outlaw

guided it up the slope into the pine-stippled heights. If the dun was wearying, he gave Killeen no indication of it. The little horse ran on stubbornly. They were closing the gap now as they wound up through the pines. The race did not always go to the swiftest.

Now as it scrambled over loose soil and small rocks, the roan slipped badly, nearly going to its haunches as it tried to continue its ascent. The man riding the horse bailed from the saddle, snatching a rifle from his scabbard, and raced toward the cover of the surrounding pine trees. Killeen did not want to come up on him too soon, too closely, and so he swung down from the dun. Carrying his Winchester, he darted into the trees which were not standing in thick clumps, but in scattered stands.

The first shot rang out from somewhere above Killeen and he drew up, rolling behind a low cluster of boulders. A second shot followed him to his position, ricocheting savagely off the rocks.

Killeen waited, eyes searching the slope above him He thought he glimpsed a shadowy figure flitting among the trees, but any shot would be too far and too uncertain. At least he had a fair idea of the ambusher's location. He crept around the stack of boulders. Cursing he drew back – he had nearly put a hand down on a rattlesnake. He waited, catching his breath, let the snake slither away and started on, now moving in a low crouch.

The outlaw leader had been circling downslope, perhaps hoping to catch up his own horse or Killeen's to continue his getaway. Perhaps it was a calculated measure – doubling back on his trail to try throwing Killeen off his track.

Killeen was having none of it.

Settling in at a notch between two split halves of a boulder he got down to the hardest assignment a fighting man can have – waiting. Half an hour on as the sun continued to beam down warmly, Killeen was thinking he might have outguessed himself. He had not caught another glimpse of the man above him. Then abruptly in a raucous black cloud, a gathering of crows rose in unison from one of the pine trees. Killeen smiled. Whatever – whoever – had startled the crows was moving in his direction, back to where the horses waited.

Killeen settled in behind the sights of the Winchester repeater, watching for movement. The desert sun was high, but it was cooler at this altitude. Nevertheless, sweat drained from Killeen's body, staining his shirt front, trickling from his armpits down across his ribs. He did not shift his position.

The crows had resettled in the trees; a light, dry breeze had begun to riffle the pines. The outlaw moved.

Killeen had to switch his sights only fractionally to settle the front bead on his man as he sprinted between the trees, and when he triggered off, the man folded up and pitched forward against the earth, his rifle falling free. Killeen waited long, slow minutes, just watching to make sure the man was not going to rise again. Then he stepped out from behind the rocks and made his way cautiously toward the bandit chief.

Steele was still alive when Killeen reached him, but he wasn't long for it. Killeen grabbed Steele's pistol, flung it away, and then helped the man to sit up against the thick trunk of a pine tree. Steele was holding his chest. Looking at Killeen he asked:

'Water?'

'Don't have any with me.'

'Oh, well,' Steele murmured. 'Probably doesn't matter. I should have stuck to gambling. . . .' Then he said nothing more.

Major Fain was seated at his desk, finishing a review of the morning reports when there was a tap at his office door and the florid face of First Sergeant Duffy appeared around the corner.

'Yes, Duffy?'

'A man to see you, Major. That railroad engineer

– Frank Ames.'

Now what? Fain wondered. He had spoken to Ames the day before when Lieutenant Calhoun had finally delivered the stolen Winchester rifles. After that the major had debriefed Calhoun. It was a rather long report the young officer had to make, but when he had finished it and turned to go he had paused and said to Fain, 'Sir, the next time I'm sent on a mission – I'd sure appreciate it if Nate Killeen is assigned to me.'

'Send the engineer in,' Fain said, and Duffy backed out of the room. In a minute Frank Ames came in, striped hat in hand.

' 'Morning, sir,' Ames said.

'Yes, Ames?' the silver-mustached officer asked patiently.

'You know that the railroad has found a new crew for the Comanche Wells station – a father and son, they are. . . .'

'Fine,' the major said with a touch of impatience. He didn't need to know about the railroad's business – just so they got through on time.

'Well, sir,' Ames said, reaching into his pocket. 'Something was left at the station with them. They were instructed to give it to me to deliver to you.' He handed over the folded sheet of paper on which was scrawled:

Major Fain, Fort Thomas.
I have advanced to Mayfield. I respectfully request a ten-day furlough beginning immediately.
Y'rs sincerely – Nate Killeen.

Ames waited for the major to say something. A smile had creased the officer's face. Ames asked: 'Everything all right, sir?'

'It seems so, Ames. It seems so. On your way out would you ask my first sergeant to come back in. A matter of some paperwork we need to do.'

The wedding between Marie Slattery and First Lieutenant Mark Calhoun was held at Marshal Slattery's house some weeks later. There was a delegation from Fort Thomas present: Major Fain, Sergeant Duffy and a few of Calhoun's other friends from the post. Also present were one Nate Killeen and Tombstone Jack, who managed to remain relatively sober throughout the ceremony. Station master Quentin Garrett and his wife were there, and a dozen or so other townspeople, including the widow of the banker Henry Crimson, whom rumor had it was soon to marry again. The future bridegroom was one Thaddeus Folger who stood at her side, beaming. Garrett was so caught up in the spirit of the day that he offered Thad Folger his old job back. . . .

Providing. . . .

But Thad had shed his old ways. He had emptied out the rest of the stolen goods in Paulsen's barn, and swore privately to Tombstone that his days as a predator were over.

Besides, the former Mrs Crimson had a good deal of her own money, wherever it had come from.

As for Nate Killeen, he was well-rested and ready to get back to work. In Mayfield he had met in passing an attractive young woman who worked in the dry goods store, but he gave no thought to settling down even on a day such as this. The long trail still held its allure; besides, he decided, these town folks seemed to lead very complicated lives.

23 4 35